Inspection of a Small Village

Connie Gault

Inspection of a Small Village

Coteau Books

Edited by Bonnie Burnard.
Cover painting, by Jane Zednik, "Inspection" 12 x 18, oil on paper, 1995.
Cover design by Catherine Bradbury.
Book design and typesetting by Ruth Linka.
Printed and bound in Canada.

The author gratefully acknowledges the financial assistance of the Saskatchewan Arts Board during the writing of this collection. She also thanks Marlis Wesseler and Dianne Warren for generously reading some of the earlier drafts of the stories.

Some of the stories in this collection have appeared in early versions in the following publications: *Canadian Fiction Magazine*, *Grain*, *Lodestone*, *NeWest Review*, and *Prairie Schooner*.

The publisher gratefully acknowledges the financial assistance of the Saskatchewan Arts Board, the Canada Council, the Department of Canadian Heritage, and the City of Regina Arts Commission.

Canadian Cataloguing in Publication Data

Gault, Connie, 1949-
Inspection of a small village

ISBN 1-55050-095-3

I. Title.

PS8563-A8445I58 1996 C813'.54 C95-920938-7
PR9199.3.G378I58 1996

Coteau Books
401-2206 Dewdney Avenue
Regina, Saskatchewan
S4R 1H3

For Bruce and Shirley.

Contents

My Star Crossed Eyes

I am an old woman now but once (and this surprises even me) I was a child. And in the way that children will, I believed I was an important person. Perhaps I should say I believed my father, who said I was important. Of course, I did not understand his motivation. I took what he said for truth.

My father told me the stars had crossed my eyes. He wanted me to wear my eye patch, which I hated. He said the stars had crossed the sky when I was born and this had given me a special gift of seeing, which I must develop. Having suffered a little the tentative feelings of being different from other children, I took to the idea of specialness with fervour. I also kept hold of an affinity for the sky and all the bodies in it that had taken such an interest in me.

By the time I was eleven, I knew my father's story was a fairy tale kind of thing, but his invention of it and the special status it had given me – in my own eyes – upheld my belief in my own importance, upheld it at least until Elena Huttala came to town and robbed me, first of my importance, then of my father, and finally of my future. I say she robbed me of my future because once my father had left us, there was no money for my education. Yet I cannot blame her. Nor can I blame my father. If she was not exactly beautiful, she was alluring. I fell in love with her myself, as a child will fall in love with someone she longs to be.

I was out walking along the railway tracks the day Elena Huttala stepped into our world. While I was walking, I was planning what I was going to say to Mrs. Knoblauch about the sky. Mrs. Knoblauch was a woman I considered very old and very wise and it was my ambition to impress her. Although it was not my only reason for thinking myself important, my vision (I thought of it as my astonishing vision) was my only talent. For the most part it was a secret talent, for the simple reason that people found it either uninteresting or scandalous, depending on how I used it. I had two ways of seeing. The first was things; this was the type of vision my father had promoted. The other was people. I believed I could see into the hearts and minds and bodies of other people. No one encouraged this. Fantasy was what they called it, and it sounded like an illness. My father had told me the story of my vision as a way to get me to wear my eye patch, but by the time Elena Huttala came to our town, Mrs. Knoblauch was the only one who fostered this talent and helped me keep it alive.

The day Elena Huttala came to town the sky was sulky. I was thinking of telling Mrs. Knoblauch that the sun was like a weak god burning behind clouds, spraying down his impotence – but I knew I'd be afraid to say it. The word impotence sounded like a challenge, and the truth was I was alarmed by that sun in that sky. The sky was too white for one thing, not bleached of colour but white inlaid or enamelled white; it was a more opaque sky than I was comfortable with. The clouds were more like big flakes of pearl than the wisps or billows I had been accustomed to. The sun was concealing its fire, but the fire could not be contained, it spewed out, it ate spokes through the enamelled sky, it sizzled down to earth. I couldn't help thinking that although it was my fondest desire, I was too small a person to live alone.

But that sky came later in the day. When Elena Huttala stepped out of the car, interrupting her journey to the city, the sky wasn't so much out of the ordinary. Maybe it was lighter than the usual sky, and the air was still. It was a hot August day in 1923. I was nowhere near when she stepped down from the car but I so often imagined her arrival – it was of such importance to me – that I can see her now as I saw her then. I can see her clearly and, it seems, with the same young inventive eyes. When I think of Elena Huttala, I am almost given over to my childhood self. And that young self, from the day she arrived until long after she left, was nearly given over to her.

This state of affairs was not entirely new to me. I had discovered at an early age that my vision could take me far enough inside another's body, heart, and mind to trick me into believing I could be that person. But I had always maintained a double vision. While usurping another's personality or circumstance, I had remained myself, standing back watching. Perhaps Elena Huttala was different, and perhaps she asserted herself more strongly, because our lives intersected in time as much as in place, because I was ready to give up my childhood and had, as yet, no alternative I liked.

She was not very old herself when she came to our town, but I guess no one had mentioned to her how young she was; she took no notice of it. Being unconcerned with her youth freed her mind for other reflections on herself that she considered more important, such as: that she was a forward-looking woman, and that she was sexy. I believe those would have been the two of prime importance, probably in reverse order.

But what do my suppositions matter – it is what I see that interests me. The car door opening, her honey-coloured hair, one bare tanned leg, then another, as she placed her feet on the running board. Her brown dress clinging damply to her thighs as she stepped down to the gravel road and looked ahead (from inside herself) and looked sexy (that was the view from the car) and thought she was on top of the world. Just moments before she'd been travelling fast down the highway in the boxy interior of a new Chevrolet; a red-haired man was driving. The car was hot, the windows were down, they were going to the city. They had a bit of a plan, or she did. He was probably more amused than purposeful. Yes, I think so. She amused him. He was older than Elena and had learned to take things as they came, especially when they came so easy. She had a bag in the back of the car, packed with things the red-haired man had given her and a few things of her own, and she had about the same proportion of ideas in her mind, although you couldn't have told her that. She was carrying along the odd idea from her father as well – also unacknowledged. For instance, she got her forward-looking attitude from him. Even though he was a man who despised his own past, whose most frequent words to her had been, "Eyes front, Elena," she didn't make a connection between his attitude and her own. When she left him behind, she thought she'd dropped him out of her life.

Her desire to be desirable was her own. Not a unique desire but it seemed in her to be uniquely strong. Or maybe it wasn't any stronger in her than in other young women, maybe it was only more evident. Her name was Elena but she had decided she wanted to be called Lee. She thought Lee sounded modern.

They had been driving fast; the roads were poor in those days and the cars were set high on their wheels, so they bounced along in the ruts and out of them, kicking up gravel, stirring up dust and generally making their presence known across the countryside. People looked up when they passed by farms and through towns. Elena Huttala rode with her right arm out the window ready to wave at people they passed. The red-haired man, whose name was Bill Longmore, tooted the horn.

After a couple of hours of this, they quieted down and Bill silently congratulated himself on picking up a woman who didn't have to talk. She didn't even seem to be thinking, which was also good. As for Elena, she was content to watch the fields jolt by and the road run toward them and disappear under the car. From time to time she speculated on what the city would look like; she had seen pictures and like a child she imagined the road terminating in a sudden conglomeration of tall buildings and streetcars. It was an exciting image; she kept it, knowing it was untrue, because it fit with the forward-looking idea of herself that she had inherited from her father.

She was riding along, looking at the road ahead from the hot black leather interior of Bill Longmore's Chevrolet, then there was a truck ahead. She was watching it in a careless sort of way when it made a left turn off the highway onto a side road. Elena Huttala turned her head and saw a town, a little town down a side road, looking silvery and soft in the distance, its houses softly shrubbed and dustily hedged and pillowed in silvery grasses. Knee-high, dry grasses, foxtails, things like that. It looked a lot like the town she'd left behind but that didn't occur to her.

"Stop," she said.

Bill braked and they fishtailed in the loose gravel. The car stalled. She hadn't spoken for miles, then said stop. A cloud of dust rose and fell around them.

When Elena Huttala opened the car door and swung her feet out, she noticed the sheen of the sun on her legs but she had no thoughts for the sun itself or the somewhat unusual whiteness of the sky. She knew exactly what she was doing and she thought she knew why. She stepped off the running board onto the gravel. She didn't say a thing. She shut the door with a smack and took off down the road. She was wearing heels that Bill Longmore had bought her of soft light brown leather with a strap near the ankle. She was ruining the shoes by walking down the gravel road. That was one thing she hadn't considered.

Walking down the road ahead of the car, ruining her shoes, Elena Huttala listened for the sound of the engine and anticipated Bill Longmore driving up beside her. She was almost at the intersection of the road into town; she thought he'd follow her down the road. There was just as good a chance he wouldn't, but she didn't think too much about that. If he followed her, her plan would be back on track, there would be other shoes. If he went, it was because he had to be on top. She turned left onto the dirt road and kept on walking. She didn't look back. The truck she'd watched had pulled into town and nothing was moving except for her and the sea of wheat on either side of the road. And the grasshoppers. They arced over the road, sometimes as many as twenty or thirty in the air at once. Their whirring filled the air. She walked through them, pretending they couldn't hit her. A blackbird sang suddenly, repeated itself and fell quiet. He hadn't started the car yet. She guessed he was considering. While she walked down the road she thought about him looking at her in her brown dress. She didn't have a thing on under her brown dress and he knew it. She thought about him growing hard looking at her. She thought about her power over him. He was the first man she'd known and she didn't realize that thing of his could grow and harden without the magic of her presence. Walking down the road thinking about him hard, she started feeling soft. She decided when he drove up beside her, she'd crawl into the back seat, she'd pull up the modest brown dress he'd made fun of but secretly liked, she'd hike it up over her knees and he'd pull over into the ditch. He'd climb right over the seat. She heard the ignition crank, the engine catch and throb. She kept on walking, maybe not so fast.

Bill Longmore sat on the main road, vibrating along with his Chev. He didn't notice she had forgotten her bag or he would have heaved it out into the ditch. She didn't think of it herself until it was too late. By then, she was halfway to the town; he was halfway to the city. She knew she wouldn't see her things again. He wasn't the type to backtrack.

It was a long, hot trek into town. She did regret what she'd done but she couldn't undo it in her mind any more than she could in fact. She told herself his tug on her had been too strong; it was a relief to have him gone.

Our town was smaller than she'd thought. Before she went into the general store – the only store – she shook out her hair and smeared her face with her fingertips. The best she could hope for was to smudge the sweat, the powder, and the dust together. She checked the buttons on the front of her dress. She sat on the bench outside the store and brushed at her shoes. Two men stood in the open door of the garage opposite, smoking and watching her.

The storekeeper was a stalwart man named Lloyd Owen. I am pleased to call him stalwart, a word I see with banners flying, even though the day Elena Huttala arrived in town he hadn't earned the title yet. The time was going to come when he'd give my mother unlimited credit, when it would be all our family had to live on and a hardship to him. Physically, he was a tall slender man, stooped in the way tall slender men are when they feel apologetic for having to look down on others. He had a wife and two daughters who worked in the store and a son who farmed just out of town and helped him with any heavy work.

He had no work for Elena Huttala. He thought she looked about fifteen and felt sorry for her. There were no businesses in the town that employed women except the cafe that was run by a Chinese family and the hotel that was run by the Fairleys. Neither needed staff. He told her he didn't think she'd find work. His son, Scott, happened to be stacking crates in the stockroom and came out front to see who was there, so he saw Elena, her first day in town. She looked about eighteen to him. She looked like a girl he'd been dreaming about, some of those nights he'd spent alone on his farm outside town. That was because of something she did when he walked out front as his father was telling her he didn't think she'd find work in the town; she raised her hand and laid the backs of her fingers against her cheek, then turned the hand and laid them on the other cheek, as if to quell a blush. As if she'd read his mind. Later he admitted he would have crossed the store and knelt at her feet if he could have acted according to his desire. He would have stroked the film of dust from her shoes. He would have laid his head against the modest brown dress and asked for her hand in marriage. He was the town's most eligible bachelor but he would have knelt on the oiled boards in front of his father and declared his love and given all his worldly possessions to touch those shoes, that dress. In fact, he did nothing. Self-preservation kept him in the shadows at the back of the store.

The store was not like other stores she'd been inside, in spite of its oiled board floor, the smell of that oil and the smell of the round of cheddar on the counter, and the smell of brown paper and string. It was different in small ways that had to do with the storekeeper, his wife and his daughters, how they thought a shelf should look, their sense of order, proportion, and colour. Subdued, she thought it, and although she looked as subdued as she could, herself, in her brown dress, she thought they would be afraid of her. When Scott Owen entered from the back of the store just as Lloyd was telling her there was no work for her in the town, she saw why they would be afraid. Her gesture then had nothing to do with modesty, it was an acknowledgement. Attracted to a man, she let him know; it was that simple. Or it seemed that simple to Elena, whose experience of being a woman seemed to have begun with her first man.

She turned and left the store. Lloyd Owen and Scott watched her through the window, expecting to see her walk past. Really, they expected to see her picked up in a car – the entrance of his son into the store had made Lloyd see Elena differently. He saw that she was older than he'd first thought; he saw that she might have driven in cars with men. They listened for the sound of a car on Main Street. She sat on the bench outside the store and wondered what she could possibly do next.

While she sat there the sun began to display itself but she didn't pay any heed; she was starting to get thirsty. The two men who were watching her from the open door of the garage across the street went inside every once in a while and brought out a cup of coffee or sometimes a dripping cup of water. She was thinking she would have to go over and ask for some when one of the men, Walter Dunn it was, started across the street with a cup in his hand. One of those shallow old speckled enamelled cups that makes coffee cool quickly and water taste colder than it does in anything else. It was a wide uneven gravel street that Walter Dunn had to cross and it was quite a feat for him to get to her without spilling the water. He was concentrating on doing it partly because it wasn't easy and partly to keep from looking too anxious to make Elena Huttala's acquaintance.

At the same time he was making his way to her, I turned onto Main Street, walking in the middle of the street with my head back and my eyes on that sun in that spectacular sky. I hadn't been the first to notice it. I'd passed Joe Lamont's house and the old bugger had been lying on a lounge chair on their front porch, staring up, and as I went on down the lane, I saw Aunt Lizzy Fairley on her knees in her garden, looking up. Once I saw that sun eating its spokes down toward us, I couldn't stop looking at it. It wasn't very bright; it hardly hurt my eyes. As I said before, it alarmed me. You couldn't see that sky without thinking something was going to happen.

I ran into Walter Dunn. He was a man as solid as thirty prosperous years could make him and I was an eleven-year-old girl. I fell down, he only spilled the entire cup of water. If I'd been a boy he'd have sworn at me; as I wasn't he bit his tongue and helped me to my feet. He dusted me off a bit roughly. I thought I might mention it to my mother, but I forgot because just then I saw Elena Huttala sitting on the bench in front of the store. The way she sat on that bench, alone and unconcerned, made me close my left eye to get her into clearer focus, and that was something I hardly ever did by then. It was a habit I'd broken because my father had said it wouldn't do to have people think I was winking at them.

Elena told fortunes by reading palms, that first day in town, sitting on the bench in front of the store. She read the palms of half the people in town. The other half were afraid, not so much to know their futures as to have their hands held in hers. The ones who had their palms read didn't say too much about it, but they acted as if they now possessed some unique knowledge that was not communicable to the uninitiated. The uninitiated became disdainful. Really, she said nothing of much significance to anyone. She met their eyes, if they would let their eyes be met, as they stepped onto the sidewalk in front of the store. If they looked at her, she said she was telling fortunes to raise a little cash. Would they like their palms read?

It started with me. I mean I gave her the idea. After our collision, Walter Dunn went back to the garage for more water even though Bob Newton was laughing at him. Bob Newton owned the garage then; he was the man who'd been watching Elena with Walter. Elena herself didn't so much as smile. She acted as if none of it had anything to do with her. I could see my only hope of getting any attention from anyone was to pretend to be hurt. Luckily, I'd scraped the palm of my right hand when I'd fallen. While Walter was out of sight, I made my way toward the store, nursing my hand and trying to squeeze out a tear or two, unsuccessfully. I had never been much of a crier. I walked up to her and held out my hand. She was a woman. I'd grown up expecting maternal solicitude wherever I found a woman.

"Yes?" she said, glancing from my hand to my face.

Walter Dunn came out of the garage then. I could hear him crunching over the gravel. She took my hand lightly in both of hers. "I see accidents," she said. She turned my hand this way and that and pulled the fingers back so the drops of blood swelled at the base of my palm and the bits of stone stood up. "I believe you're prone to them," she said.

She rose to receive Walter Dunn and his cup of water. Had I been a few years older, I would have realized my audience with her was over. Maybe I did know it and chose to act under cover of my age. I plunked myself down on the wooden sidewalk at her feet.

She didn't know a lot about reading palms or telling fortunes. She'd had her palm read at a fair that had gone the rounds of some of the bigger towns the summer before. She hadn't paid much attention to the woman who'd told her fortune; she hadn't believed a word of it and couldn't have repeated any of it two days later. There were lines that were supposed to mean things; she remembered a heart line and a life line but not which was which. What she did was she held each hand in turn and stared intently at the palms. Sometimes those lines and their crossings stirred her imagination. More often the calluses, the rashes, or the bitten nails gave her clues; more often than that, the temperature of the hands, their moistness or dryness, the degree of tremor, told her what to say. It wasn't too hard to understand enough of people's lives to impress them. Also, she was charming, she sat straight and relaxed on the bench in front of the store window, and did not smile at them. She took them more seriously than they were able to take themselves. They were new citizens of a town not a dozen years old. They had no history behind them other than the culture and geography they'd given up in order to settle in their new home and, I guess, the stories they'd been able to garner about the Great War. They didn't value the stories of their pioneers and only the influenza epidemic had tested them. She knew all that. She didn't talk about dark strangers or mysterious letters from across the ocean. She talked about the things that were going to test them, the things that would expose their weakness or make them strong. She talked about land, about crops, about rainfall, harvest, machinery, horses and automobiles, the price of wheat, the price of eggs and butter, about fashion sense, housekeeping and gardening, even, vaguely, about sexual prowess and fertility, and she connected all these with their abilities. She made it seem that everything in their futures was dependent on their individual abilities, their intelligence and creativity and most of all their willpower. They weren't exactly sure, though, whether it was the things she said to them or something less definable that made them feel more powerful when she let go their hands. Her body was unusually present to them; they sensed that, but it confused them. They preferred not to think of it. They thought of themselves as simple people and she was, they reminded themselves, just a girl.

Walter Dunn was the first person whose palm she read, after she drank his water. He asked her what she was doing in town and before you knew it she was foretelling a car for every family and a boom for garage owners who had been smart enough to get into the business early. Then she found out she had the wrong man. Bob Newton owned the garage. Walter Dunn worked as an administrator for the Rural Municipality and just passed time helping Bob Newton hold up the garage walls. She switched to talking about men who were smart enough to get an education, men who earned the respect of others by holding important, responsible public positions and she thought she saw (in his thumb, I think it was) the sign of a man of passion.

After she finally finished with Walter Dunn I begged her to read my palm. I knew there had to be more than accidents in my future and she might have made a mistake about that; she hadn't spent any time at all thinking about me. She said she couldn't, my hand had been damaged and the reading wouldn't be clear.

"Do my left hand," I said.

But I wasn't left-handed. She said it wouldn't work.

"What if I only had one hand?" I asked.

"Then I'd feel sorry for you," she said.

I said I'd get money but nothing would move her. I had to watch everyone else step up with their money and their undamaged hands. It was unusual and difficult for me to stand to the side. Besides owning the distinction of an astonishing vision, I was the first child born in our town and occasionally something was made of the fact. I was also the oldest in my family and the caretaker of the six children who had been born to my mother and father since my birth, the most recent only weeks before Elena Huttala came to town. I was being raised to be a mother; it was my destiny and I was receiving ample training. I had grown used to assuming responsibility and to being treated with some deference, yet recently something had been happening to me. It seemed to be connected to the birth of my new sister, which had meant even more responsibility had fallen on me. In the midst of my busiest moments, which had formerly made me feel proud, I felt my mind fly away from my brothers and sisters, fly out of the house or yard. I watched my hands wiping a nose or drying dishes as if they were someone else's hands. And then I felt a bursting need to slap, to break, to run. I'd started slipping away so my mother couldn't ask me to do the next thing. Instead of making me feel better, being away from home made me feel worse; it was hard to go back and never be alone. It was hard to go back and find my mother angry because she'd needed me. I wanted to slip back into the house as I'd slipped out, unnoticed, and lie in a cool, dark, empty room that was mine alone, on an unshared bed. I had begun to fantasize strange turnings of events that would end with me living in a house alone, or at least in a quiet house.

I suppose it was natural, given this situation, and listening to Elena talk to one person after another about their futures, and watching them being attracted to her, that I would begin a new fantasy. I knew as soon as it entered my mind that the fantasy had some basis in reality, in observations I had made about my father and pretty girls. Possibly I was doing more forecasting than Elena, and only perceived it as a kind of daydream arranging of the future. I could see it clearly. In my daydream I convinced my father to have his palm read. He was to fall in love with Lee (the name she was telling people to call her by) and leave my mother. Then Lee and my father would skip town, taking me with them. At the end of this journey, which I envisioned as a flight – an actual flying over fields and roads, the three of us in a V formation, until the fields and roads turned unfamiliar – was a cool dark quiet house in which there was a cool dark quiet room for me. I knew this fantasy was flawed and childish but I also knew I wasn't going to give it up. It was one of those ideas that arrives fully formed and is attractive in part because it seems to require almost no effort. I even allowed myself the luxury of feeling sorry for my mother and my sisters and brothers, thinking about them being abandoned by my father, realizing that they were not as special to him as I knew myself to be. At the same time, my fantasy was nothing I wanted to act on. I did not think I had any intention in mind when I went and found my father and told him about Elena Huttala who was reading palms on the main street of our town.

My father worked for Jack Newton at the Pool elevator. I wasn't allowed to go inside but I could stand at the door and yell into the grain dust if my mother needed my father for anything. While Elena read Aunt Lizzy Fairley's palm, I took off for the elevator. Aunt Lizzy was over eighty. I figured I wouldn't miss much.

My father was a restless man. He said he couldn't come just then to hear his fortune but I could see I'd intrigued him. He was just the opposite of the people who were afraid to have their hands held by Elena. I'd known he would be. I didn't describe her much. I said she was young, she was wearing a brown dress, and in my opinion she had nothing on under it. He pretended to be shocked and cross at me for talking that way. I started to explain that I'd watched her closely from my position at her feet. I knew he'd stop me before I could get into details, before I could tell him I'd seen the shadow of a loose breast through her dress and the round smooth roll of her thigh and her bare legs. He didn't need to hear the evidence.

Before long my father found an opportunity to take a break from work and do an errand at the store. I hadn't been back at my station on the sidewalk more than ten minutes when he showed up at the corner of the street. Elena was reading Bob Newton's palm. He'd been watching everybody else all afternoon and had finally got up the nerve. He had a bright pink smudge across the top of both cheeks by the time my father strolled up. Elena was able to use her wisdom to foretell, once again, and more appropriately this time, a car for every family. Bob Newton wasn't that used to being told he was smart and he took to it. My father interrupted the flow for Bob. Elena ignored him, but Bob couldn't. He started shuffling his feet and saying, "Uh." I guess it was the thought of another man hearing the intimate exchange between a fellow and his fortuneteller. He hadn't minded me. Nobody had minded me or even seemed to see me except some of the teenagers who'd looked at me as if they'd seen an insect.

Before Bob Newton could leave and Lee could turn her attention our way, I opened my mouth to say something to my father. I don't remember what it was I wanted to say. He was standing over me. He put his hand out to stop my words. His fingers rayed down like the spokes of the sun had, and that reminded me I hadn't noticed the sky when I'd gone to the elevator to get him, so it must have been more normal. Where I was, in front of the store, I couldn't see the sun unless I stepped out into the middle of the street and I didn't plan to do that. I didn't plan to miss a word between my father and Lee.

What I planned didn't mean a thing. I got to see a look pass between the two of them while Bob Newton was backing off. At first I thought it was a look like a promise, but it wasn't. It was a recognition look. Neither Elena Huttala nor my father were people for making promises. Which was just as well, I suppose, since neither were people for keeping them. So I saw the look. But as for watching and listening and interpreting subsequent looks – that was denied me. My father, looking at Lee (not looking at me), said, "Go home and give your mother a hand." An interesting choice of words, I thought, but I knew he wouldn't appreciate my pointing it out. I also knew it would do me no good to wheedle. I shifted further down the sidewalk, hoping they'd get so involved in one another he'd forget about me. A moment or two passed. Maybe he counted to ten. He used to tell me that when he got to be an old man and lost all his senses he'd still remember to count to ten if anyone mentioned my name. "Go," he said, and this time he reached back and picked up my collar. It was too much like being picked up by the scruff of the neck for me to leave with dignity. I jerked out of his grip. I was already crying when I started yelling at him for having so many kids and making me look after them. It was so outrageous a thing to say that he laughed and shook his head and for a minute I almost thought he was proud of me. I thought if he was, even Lee might be impressed. But he stopped laughing, his face straightened, and he pointed the way home. Didn't say a thing. So I had to go.

I had to imagine what passed between them. It wasn't any fun, because when I was walking away I heard them both laugh and I couldn't help thinking they were laughing at me.

After supper Elena Huttala was still sitting on the bench in front of the store. The disdainful uninitiated, especially the women, became vocal. Lloyd Owen mentioned to his wife and daughters that they might consider asking her what her plans were. His daughters didn't answer. They were miffed because their mother hadn't let them have their palms read. Margaret Owen answered. She said one thing she'd learned from running a store a lot of the years of her life was to mind her own business. She also said that she was surprised to see her son still in town when he must have work to do on his farm. So Scott drove his horses and wagon back to the farm.

Elena Huttala showed no signs of leaving the bench. The women of the town knew they couldn't allow her to sleep there overnight. This was not a matter of her safety. The weather was warm and no one would harm her, but it wouldn't have been decent. The women of the town discussed what was to be done. Eventually they consulted Mrs. Knoblauch, who was always consulted eventually because she was thought to have common sense. Mrs. Knoblauch was probably the only person in town who had remained unaware of Elena's presence. She had picked up her mail and the day's groceries in the morning and sat in her back yard in the shade of her caragana hedge all the afternoon.

The women of the town were used to asking for Mrs. Knoblauch's advice and opinions; what she gave them was often unusual but useful. They knew almost nothing about her. She had come to town, alone, eight or nine years before, in answer to an advertisement in a city newspaper of a house for sale. She'd bought the house, one of fewer than twenty in the town and the only one vacant because the town was new and most people didn't think of moving away, they expected more would be moving in. They assumed Mrs. Knoblauch was a widow. The most they knew of her in the way of biography they'd gleaned when they'd asked her if she agreed it was true that the difference between a happy woman and an unhappy woman was that the former had married a good man. Mrs. Knoblauch had said she didn't see how it could be true, when she herself had been happy most of her life.

Mrs. Knoblauch was my favourite person in the world after my father. Until the day Elena Huttala came to town, my best fantasy had been that she would see my dilemma and invite me to live with her. I had never been inside her house but I had seen inside and I knew it would be a dark, cool, quiet house. Whenever Mrs. Knoblauch met me, she always asked: what have you seen today? Always. Because she knew I was proud of my one and only talent. So I loved her, even though I was afraid of her as well. I wanted her to love me too, so I practiced my answers all the time, I tried to make them mature and unusual. I tried to look at the most mundane things with eyes that had seen much and could compare and evaluate and still see something new. All for Mrs. Knoblauch. She never commented, but sometimes she looked happy at what I'd said and once in a while she looked as if she'd seen it too. Once tears came to her eyes and she put her hand on my shoulder and said, "Child." And that was my happiest moment.

The day Elena Huttala came to town was the day the word impotence came into my mind as a way to describe the sun. Sometimes words like that popped into my mind without my knowing exactly what they meant; they were words I knew vaguely from books. I remember I was afraid to say the word out loud because I suspected it meant weakness and I knew I often wanted things to be weak so I could feel strong. It didn't matter anyway because I never got the chance to say anything about that sun to Mrs. Knoblauch. Right that day her life got filled up with Elena Huttala. And after that day, though she still asked me what I'd seen and I still answered, no matter how good my answers were, I never thought she listened the same.

The women of the town were surprised when Mrs. Knoblauch took Elena in. They were used to Mrs. Knoblauch surprising them, but they felt her offer to share her home was truly out of character. She had not invited any of them into her house for so much as a cup of tea. Although she was quite old, over seventy, they didn't think she needed a housekeeper. Yet sight unseen, and with no recommendation – because they knew so little to tell her – she welcomed the girl into her house. What they had been able to tell her was hardly enough for even a good Christian (which Mrs. Knoblauch was not) to go on, which was why they had hesitated in offering her a place for the night themselves, although one of them would have done so if it had become absolutely necessary. The women wanted to fetch Elena Huttala and introduce her, but Mrs. Knoblauch said they were to send her along on her own and tell her to wait in the back yard.

That was how it happened that Elena stood in a back yard hedged with caraganas, bareheaded, in her brown dress, and Mrs. Knoblauch watched her from a kitchen window. Mrs. Knoblauch's strong old hand gripped the window sill. The caragana pods were popping. They snapped and flew from the bushes. Elena flinched, one pod had hit her on the cheek. It left a red mark on her cheek. Crack! Snap! The kitchen window was open, but Mrs. Knoblauch couldn't hear the sound; she was remembering it, remembering sitting in the shade of her hedge that afternoon, hearing the small explosions. The pods shot from their branches. Elena stood still, surrounded on three sides. Above her was an unnaturally pearly sky brightened by a setting sun, behind her a house she had never entered, the house of an old woman she had not met.

Mrs. Knoblauch moved to her screened door. The screen was loosely tacked and a light breeze blew a pulse inward, then out, every once in a while. A puff of dust rose from the screen each time it stirred. Elena Huttala stood in the back yard waiting for her future to catch up to her. She didn't realize she was waiting. She thought she was only stopping – here, now, in a strange yard where dusty caragana hedges were assaulting her – yet without thinking much about it she was also aware of feeling that no other time or place existed. It was a curious feeling, as close as she had come to the recollection of being unborn.

Then the screened door opened. She turned, faced the house – and colour. A row of hollyhocks grew against the house, their big leaves a bright green, their flowers pink, wine red, maroon. An old woman stood in front of the hollyhocks; the blossoms rose two feet higher than her head. The sun was lowering itself through the mauve sky. It happened to be sitting on Mrs. Knoblauch's roof when Elena turned to the house, to the hollyhocks and the old woman standing in the doorway. And they were all bright and dark at the same time, lit on their edges, dark at their centres because the sun was sitting on the roof. She could not see Mrs. Knoblauch's face. She looked into the sun. It was a blinding hole in the sky. For several seconds afterwards she saw green spots wherever she looked, then the spots turned pink and finally they faded and she was able to go to meet Mrs. Knoblauch.

The first time I saw Elena Huttala, I thought by the way she sat on the store bench, loose and unconcerned with everything around her, that she was alone and comfortable with it. But it turned out that wasn't the case. It turned out she was the child of a mother who had died at her birth and a father who had raised her with the expectation that she would leave. She was accustomed to being alone, that was all. What she wanted was another thing.

The sky was wild with colour when she stepped up to meet Mrs. Knoblauch, apricot and violet and baby blue and gold, and it was no ordinary sunset, striped across the west. The colours were reflected all around and when the sun dipped further, the full bowl of the sky turned mother of pearl. It became a more tender sky than any of us had seen before. I think it was the coincidence of Mrs. Knoblauch inviting her and the sky being so tender that made Elena Huttala decide to stay. That sky. I can see it still. My vision has not been impaired by age, though I no longer consider it astonishing.

That sky. All day the people of the town who thought of themselves as realists had been predicting hail. The sunset shut them up. The superstitious held to their belief that the day had been in all respects lucky and the future would confirm it. Then there were some of us (I can't have been the only one) who'd just as soon have forgotten we'd ever seen that sky. We were the ones who thought we could arrange the future and even rearrange it when it didn't suit our plans.

Postscript

There is always something new to learn. This is one of the real reasons to go on living, although what I will do, what anyone does with the accumulated knowledge, I'm not sure. Still, it seems a plus, to learn something new, another check on the chart, an increase in the score. And what have I learned? Simply this: of all the people I have known, there was only one I did not presume to know through the eyes of my imagination. That was Mrs. Knoblauch. Her hand on that window sill was as close as I could get. Although I badly wanted to live in her house, for I hoped it would provide the peace I needed, I never stepped inside. She remained – and remains still – a mystery to me. A challenge. I am no respecter of persons, that is clear. Perhaps I should take her on. She can be my last and most astonishing self.

A Burning House

A house was on fire. A man and a woman were standing in the prairie farmyard watching it burn to the ground. It was a beautiful spring day, the end of April, 1949, and it was warm enough they didn't need coats. She wore a long sweater with pockets for the things she was always picking up and he wore one of the generic light jackets that had hung for years at the front door of the big house. The jacket smelled of smoke before he reached the fire because his son had worn it last.

Bert timed the burning. Twenty-three minutes from the second Orillia noticed the smoke until the studs and the doorframes lay crossed over one another, glowing dull red in the weak afternoon sun, and he could get close enough to drizzle water around the edges. Another hour, fourteen minutes, before he was satisfied it was out.

The fire began with smouldering and smoke and it would end with ashes. But now it was burning. Not ten yards from the dugout, but what good did that do, with only the two of them to fight it. Flames were jumping out from nowhere, flaring bright and disappearing, bursting up here, running off there, climbing here, falling there, and Bert was hopping mad. He was a small man, short and round-bellied and red-headed, although his hair was lightened now with grey, and he was literally hopping like one of the fat flames leaping along the window sill, where he'd thrown the one pail of water he'd attempted. He was hopping mad, because he'd built this house and there wasn't a damn thing he could do but watch it burn and he had farmed this land for so long and raised five children with no backtalk allowed, ever, and got so far on his temper with everyone and everything except rainfall, grasshoppers, and the price of grain that he'd come to think if the latter were God's territory, the rest was his. And now the first house he'd built, with his own hands, no help from a single soul, every single nail hammered in with his own hands, was burning down. It was only a shack with one room partitioned into two and until Duncan, his son, and Duncan's new wife, Merle, moved in, it had been used for fifteen years as a granary, but that was beside the point. It was burning down. He'd built it with no knowledge, no plans, no skill. He'd built it without even a memory of how such a house should be, because he'd never lived in a one-room shack.

"Careless! Careless!" he yelled over and over, wearing a path the length of the little house into the thin old grass of the summer before. "Careless!" he yelled and pulled out his pocket watch to check the time again. How long would it take to undo a man's work? He backed away from the fire at the thought the heat might hurt his watch. He had told everyone who would listen that his father had given him that watch the day he left England. He had not told the story so often he believed it himself. At eighteen, a short, red-headed young man of no consequence, he left his country. It was true his father raised his head from his work when Bert took his leave. "I won't shake your hand, Bert," he said. Not to get him bloody. His father was a butcher in Greenwich, where time began and ended. Fitting that he would give his son a watch to send him on his way to Canada. But he wasn't a man to do the fitting thing or he would not have married Bert's stepmother and brought their family down even lower than it had started.

Bert might have gone into a pawnshop and got himself a good quality secondhand watch for a decent price. He could have pretended it was a watch his father had been given by his father on a similar occasion signalling his manhood. But Bert thought it would have been more fitting, on his setting out for the new world, to get a new watch. At a jeweller's in Oxford Street in London, the day before he took the boat, he bought himself a gold pocket watch and a chain. It cost him half his savings and he was able to buy less land because of it, land that might have done him good in later years, but he wasn't going to leave England without a family heirloom for the son he would have. He'd experienced how a family could be brought down through poor connections, imprudent spending, self-indulgent eating and drinking, and general carelessness. Leaving England, he was embarking in the other direction.

Nearly fifty years he'd worked to raise his family above the level of a butcher married to a careless woman. And now his own son, his only son, his unemployed son, was married to a careless woman.

"Careless!" he yelled at Orillia, trying to see into her eyes.

In all the years he'd lived with her, she'd looked directly at him maybe twice. She wasn't about to start now. He could rage all he liked. He'd married her for her caution and they both knew it. He could yell "careless" all he liked. He'd never get agreement from her. In fact, her opinion, which would never get past her lips, was less charitable than "careless." Her opinion was more suspicious, knowing, and, she was certain, true. It was no accident this house was burning.

Very still, Orillia stood, watching the fire, with her rounded shoulders and her sunken chest and her pursed lips, very still and conscious of the pale empty sky and the mild wind that was blowing the moisture out of the land and the passage of the sun across their world. Conscious in a way Bert was not. She had no need of a gold watch to tell her how the minutes swallowed the day or to prove it hadn't been wasted while consumed. She'd learned to be quiet and still at an early age and to accept passion in others with a distant appreciation. She could enjoy even her husband's anger, and this fire – this fire that Merle had certainly set – warmed her. She appreciated the impulse as action. All action anticipated possibility, this she knew. Of course Merle had set fire to the house – against the possibility of return. And no small satisfaction for Orillia. She wanted Merle gone, even at the price of losing Duncan. So she had it both ways, knowing Merle was gone for good and celebrating her daughter-in-law's triumph. For Orillia was separated enough from her feelings to admire the younger woman's nerve. It was a fine way to say no, though it wasn't Orillia's way.

There was Bert, jumping around, yelling "careless" when it was Merle's caring that was burning the house down. If Orillia had cared more, she might have changed their lives. She might have insisted on giving up the farm. She hadn't minded the loneliness, she'd welcomed it, or the hard work, she was used to that, but she resented getting nowhere – just scraping by. She might have pushed Bert to move into town. His father had trained him as a butcher. Orillia could have lived as a butcher's wife. Although it seemed less genteel than a florist's daughter, it could hardly be more strenuous work. She had worked in the greenhouse in Toronto from the time she was twelve, lugging potted plants and shrubs and buckets of long-stemmed roses in water, cold water, her hands in and out of cold water all day long, aching then as they ached now with arthritis. She'd never told Bert how hard she'd worked as a child. He'd been uncharacteristically silent about the butcher shop, too, but she'd known he'd never go back to that work. He'd lost half his thumb at it and still, when he carved a roast, he held his left hand on top of the carving fork, well above the knife. It was one of the things that endeared him to her. She was not so completely cold that she could live her marriage through without finding some things in her husband to love.

When the fire was out, they went into their house and Orillia made lunch. After lunch Bert went out to the barn and she had a bath and washed her hair. Bert stayed in his smoky clothes until the end of the day. They went to bed that night not much changed except Bert felt more strongly than usual that there was a force in the universe against him and Orillia slipped a little rum in his postum and offered to rub his back, which he accepted.

In town, too, there was need for solicitude. Merle's sister Norrie had her nose out of joint. That's the way Kay, who worked in the store with Norrie, put it. According to Kay, Norrie's nose got out of joint whenever Merle was in town, even for the briefest visit. It had been brief this time. Duncan and Merle hadn't told a soul they were leaving the farm, just drove into town in Duncan's old Ford with all their wedding gifts from eight months ago and their baby who was born a few months earlier than she should have been.

"Oh my God," Norrie said when she saw them pull up in front of the store with their mattress strapped to the roof.

"Don't worry," Merle said, before she was even out of the car. "We're not moving back." She handed the baby to Norrie and stepped out into the rutted street in her black and white spectator pumps. She was wearing a black and white checked skirt, a black blazer with velveteen lapels and a yellow nylon blouse. Beside her, Norrie looked twice as plump as usual and three times as dowdy.

"Love your hair, Merle," Kay was saying before Merle had reached the screen door. "It's a perm, isn't it?" Merle's hair was black and bushy with tiny curls. She wore it brushed back off her face and long, down to her shoulders. It was thick and shiny and picked up the light and jostled it around her face when she walked. She seemed more alive than other people, at least to Kay.

On the store step, Merle paused to light a cigarette and look over her shoulder at Duncan who was leaning on his car, talking to Norrie. He was a handsome man, took after his mother. In more ways than one. Kay held the door open, Merle went inside and bought a package of Black Cats and a bottle of milk.

Kay rang up the sale. "So, what's up?" she whispered, although they were alone in the store. Merle just smiled, picked up her bag, and went out to the car. She gave Norrie a kiss on the cheek and they took off.

They drove up the street to her mother's place. That much Kay could see from the screen door and relay to Norrie. Norrie said she could have figured that. She broke off a length of string from the roll above the till and tied it into knots, staring toward the back of the store. Kay swept the floor for the third time that day. The good thing about spring was that the wind blew dust inside and customers brought grit in on their shoes so there was always something to sweep. It had been more fun for Kay when Merle had worked in the store.

Norrie knotted her string and thought about Duncan, the perfect husband, and little Cathleen, the perfect baby, until Mrs. Huber came in for some sliced ham for her supper and both clerks rushed to wait on her.

The clothespins clacked into the basket and the long dry grass rasped as Helen kicked the basket along, dropping in clothespins, dropping in blouses and slips, bras and underpants, and nighties and vests. It was a perfect day for drying and the clothes smelled more like spring than spring itself, but Helen was not enjoying the experience. Her daughter had left her weary. So often Merle did that to her. It was because she was gone so soon after she arrived and left her mother with the feeling she could never keep up – and never had. Merle was the youngest of eleven, so perhaps Helen could have forgiven herself, but it wouldn't have occurred to her to spend time as the object of her own concern. She had gotten so used to thinking about her children, she was too old now to think about herself. So she worried about Merle, the baby, grown up before her time. Married, with a baby of her own, at nineteen. And she worried about Norrie, at twenty-one fast becoming the old maid. Still living with her mother. And upset, no doubt in a way she couldn't describe, over Merle's visit and departure.

When the last vest collapsed into the basket, Helen looked down the road past the two elevators as if she thought she might see Duncan's car heading back this way, although she knew they were gone and she was left with Norrie's discontent. The clothesline swayed. She looked up to see a blackbird a few feet away, swinging with the line. Two blackbirds made a nest every spring in her caragana hedge. She hoped it was the same couple every year; she hoped there was such a thing as fidelity.

She took the wash into the house, which was too big now for just Norrie and her. Once it had held all her children and two or three boarders. Sometimes even her husband. Now the rooms gaped, the beds made up and never slept in. She sat at the kitchen table folding the clothing that was left for her to launder. Something was going on with Merle, something more exciting than moving south to Kerrody. She'd made some decision. Helen had tried to give her children ways to guide themselves when decisions had to be made, some solid moral information. She wanted them to know there were right ways to act, but the truth was she was pretty tired by the fourth baby and had completely lost track by the tenth of what she had told them and what she'd left out. Merle had raised herself, as far as Helen could tell. Except for the day Will left. That day she'd needed a mother.

He called them out of school. Knocked on the door of the one-room schoolhouse and demanded to see his children. Eight of the students were his, a third of the school. The teacher, a frightened girl not much over twenty herself, led them out. It was a cold day in November, the kind of weather you call bitter. The children shivered because they hadn't thought to put on coats. They lined up across the school step, naturally, from the youngest to the oldest. Merle was six, her eldest sister was seventeen, in grade twelve. It was the middle of the Depression, but the children didn't know that. They knew only that they were poor. Not as badly off as the Hutterite kids who brought beet and lard sandwiches for lunch, thank God, but nearly.

He said he'd die if he had to spend another winter in Saskatchewan. He said he was moving to Ontario. "Goodbye and good luck," he said. He turned and walked away without a look back and none of them had seen him again. They assumed he'd lived, and even prospered, once he'd left Saskatchewan, where the air was too dry and the weather too cold. For his asthma.

Merle came to her mother that night. "Will you be leaving, too?" she asked, matter-of-factly, flatly.

What an old little girl you are, Helen thought. She said to her, "No, I will not be leaving. Thank you for asking, Merle, but I intend on staying."

The next day Merle had to travel to the neighbouring town by train to visit her sister-in-law Cathleen, who looked after her whenever Helen was called away to attend to a birth. Helen was the district midwife, trained by her mother back in Ontario to deal with the old curse: in sorrow bring forth children. There were two men on the train who were drinking buddies of Will's. They teased Merle about her father. They said now that her father was gone, her mother wasn't married anymore, and they'd be coming around. Maybe one of them would be her father soon. By the time she reached the station, she was nearly in a fit. She would not cry in front of the men. Cathleen, who had come to meet her at the station, saw her get off the train red-faced and stern with her back as straight and her head as high as a six-year-old can carry it. She walked with Cathleen to her house and threw the fit as soon as she got inside. A few days later, when Helen was back home, Cathleen travelled with Merle and had a long talk with her mother. When she left, Helen brought her youngest daughter into her bedroom.

"Merle," she said. "I have something for you. Do you see these rings I'm wearing? This is a wedding band. It means I'm married. As long as I wear it, no one else can be your father. This ring...." she drew off her engagement ring with the tiny ruby and the diamond chips. "This is yours." She put it on Merle's finger. It slid around, the stones turned downward.

"It's too big for you now," Helen said. "I'll keep it for you till you're older."

Helen had thought she'd give the ring to Merle on her wedding day, but Merle had seemed so young and unhesitating. With a husband barely snared and a baby on the way. Helen had not wanted to remind her of her father and Merle had not asked. Again today she'd thought she might have got it out and put it on Merle's finger, since she was moving for the first time quite far from home, a day's journey away. But Merle hadn't stayed long enough for them to get used to one another again, not long enough for them to be able to say anything to one another that would mean something, mark an occasion such as giving a gift promised long ago to a child who needed promises.

While he drove with the windows half down at his wife's request – for the smell of new grass and in spite of the dust – Duncan watched Merle feed Cathleen her bottle. At her mother's house she'd boiled the milk and the bottles and nipples and packed them in the baby's bag. If she'd taken the time to do it at home before they'd left, they wouldn't have had to buy the milk. But she was eager to be gone, to get on the road, so he said nothing to her about the expense. Although they had very little to live on, he would not be like his father, nagging over every penny. They had the money he'd earned shingling the Musgraves' roof and if that didn't last until he got a paycheck, something would come up. That was Merle's phrase: something will come up. She was singing about care and woe. What was the song – "Bye Bye, Blackbird."

"Your mother was saying her blackbirds are back again this year." So often his words came out with a formality he'd have liked to eradicate.

An inappropriate politeness, bequeathed to him by his mother. It made him feel like blushing, even in front of his wife.

Merle blew him a saucy kiss.

He was old-fashioned, that was the thing, and she was a modern girl. But she forgave him his occasional awkwardnesses, those times he felt so transparently out of step. She even implied she found them charming. Rather than loving her less for having had to marry her, he loved her more. He had an instinct, however, that told him he'd be better off keeping her guessing about that. She expected him to be a responsible husband and father, that much was clear, but clearer still was her great desire to make a game of things. She hadn't liked the farm, she'd found it boring. She was a town girl. She wasn't the first person he'd met who thought having fun was a goal in life, but she was the first who'd made him feel it with her. He understood now what a serious life he'd led and why he'd never quite fit in although people had seemed to like him well enough. Until he met Merle, he'd never known how to have a good time. She'd had to teach him.

He'd joined the air force when he turned eighteen, the last year of the war. Of course, he didn't know when he joined that it would be over soon, so he chose carefully. The army was out of the question. He was willing to die for his country if he had to but he did not believe he would be able to watch others die. He had the misfortune to faint at the sight of blood, a reaction that brought derision from his father and tight-lipped concern from his mother. How would a man get on in the world if he could not bear to see anyone hurt? The navy, too, was impossible. He'd never been on a boat bigger than a rowboat, never been near a body of water bigger than a pond. So he'd joined the airforce and trained as a radio operator. If his plane was shot out of the sky, he figured he'd die quickly, without seeing too many others go with him.

The war was over before he finished training. He'd made it as far from the farm as Halifax and there celebrated the end of a conflict he barely understood. When he got his discharge, he went home to take over the family farm as he'd been raised to do. His plan was to marry eventually, once he'd built a new house on the other side of the trees from his parents' house, where the land dipped down to the dugout. He was going to plant more trees and gardens, extending the work his father had started to civilize the landscape. His father had planted more trees than most of his neighbours. Besides their huge vegetable garden, Bert had put in, among the trees, clumps of irises and day lilies, and between the house and the trees, beds of perennials he fussed over in the evenings when the day's hard work had left him tired but restless.

Duncan had not planned to clean out his father's bachelor shack, which had been used fifteen years, at least, as a granary, and carry his wife across its threshold. But Merle had taught him that life could be good without being planned.

Duncan and Merle and Cathleen drove south in their loaded down car, a cloud of dust veiling them from the eyes of farmers in fields and housewives at their kitchen windows. Behind them their house was burning but Duncan was innocent of that knowledge and Merle could not be sure. She thought it more likely the old sofa had smouldered a while and gone out on its own. Still, she had an image of a house burning in her mind.

Duncan was happy. A lot of wives would have preferred the security of the farm, even if they hadn't liked it, to setting out to make their own way in the world. But Merle was ready for anything. She believed in him. She sat beside him with the sleeping baby in her arms and her eyes forward, watching the road come toward her. Briefly, he pictured his parents standing side by side in their yard, in their private silences, his mother maintaining hers like a duty, his father shocked into his by Duncan's leaving. He felt uneasy, reminded of them, but after all, he and Merle were nothing like his father and mother. He could do anything he wanted with Merle beside him. And if things didn't work out, they could always change their minds and go back.

Inspection of a Small Village

In a room defined by tables and windows the adulteress sits at her task. She has set herself the task to occupy her mind. The room is at the provincial archives; the adulteress is waiting for a folder of information on the town in which she was born. She has decided to stop treating herself like someone who may break with any breath she takes, but she holds herself delicately without realizing what she is doing and she sits very straight, with her hands in her lap and her head just so on her neck.

A slight young man slides the folder across the table toward her. He turns and disappears behind a swinging door without a word. This is a quiet room. Any words that are spoken by the half-dozen people distributed among the tables (with maximum space between them) are quiet words.

The folder contains the archives' local histories clippings file for the town in which she was born. Of the four items in the file, only one interests her enough that she picks it up and reads it. She holds the few pages of the badly typed report up to the fluorescent light that blankets the room, that cancels the light from the windows. She reads the words over and over and wills them to replace her thoughts. This is her task, this expulsion of her thoughts. It's a task appropriate to her dilemma, which is not so much that of being an adulteress as that of being sorry she is herself. She is young and has come against the fact of herself, a person born here, now. She thinks if she were a person born there, then, everything would be different. Given a choice, she'd be born French. Even better, she'd be born in a French movie. Those people really don't give a damn.

Report on a Systematic Inspection of the Village of Kerrody July 8, 1958

Kerrody is a small thriving Village, busy by virtue of its central location in the southwest sector of Health Region No. 2. With an estimated population of 310, there are 119 houses standing and 5 new buildings under construction. Most of the single dwellings are small and well-maintained. This pleasant Village has no slum area to speak of, no corrupting influences. The outhouses are in good repair.

The report was written by the doctor who was the Regional Medical Health Officer at the time. Likely he had no resemblance to the man the adulteress pictures; she sees a man with his elbows on the table at the Kerrody hotel and his head in his hands. A conscientious man. It is Dr. Tolley she sees with his head in his hands. The adulteress has given her medical health officer the name Tolley because that is the name of the man who has made her heart sing. She doesn't really see him sitting at the table with his head in his hands so much as she feels the presence of his body, and "heart sing" isn't the euphemism she first thought. She can't quite erase it.

Dr.Tolley is sitting in the Kerrody hotel eating a chicken sandwich. He's not sitting with his head in his hands. Not yet. He has a report to write. A report that looks like seersucker from the sweat on his hands. No, he's not anxious yet. It's hot. It's a very hot day but his hands don't sweat.

Dr. Tolley eats his sandwich and begins his report. He is new at his job but already he is determined to work as he goes while in the field and to spend as much time as possible with his wife when he's home. If Dr. Tolley is ever inclined to be smug it is on two accounts, his efficiency and his great good fortune in marriage. He is humble enough to realize that neither have come to him through his own efforts to attain them. Rather, they have been by-products of his attempts to overcome his one real weakness, his fear that he isn't good enough. He fears not being good enough in his work and with women, and for the same reason: he harbours a slight but seemingly irremediable aversion to the human body. He became a physician to conquer the body and, like others equally pretentious, he has failed. The body, in all the thousands of manifestations that have passed before his eyes and under his hands, in spite of passing before his eyes and under his hands, has gone on being corrupted and insulted by disease and injury and abuse. The body in its most pristine forms displays its ugly potential. His wife has sensed his dilemma and protects him. She never dresses or undresses in front of him and always slips between their sheets in attire no one would remark on if the house caught fire and she had to stand on the lawn with their neighbours in the middle of the night watching it burn.

The adulteress tries to focus again on the words in the report, where no one's wife is mentioned. But the man named Tolley lingers. How has he made her heart sing? Only by wanting her body and by being unable to keep her from knowing. That's all it takes to make her heart sing, to set her mind ticking, timed for any moment, just say the word, look the look. Or say nothing, look nothing: think and she'll know.

Her doctor's head is in his hands. No, not yet. He is sitting with his pen poised, going over his thoughts. And his thoughts are all of the town in which the adulteress was born. That morning Dr. Tolley walked up and down the back alleys of Kerrody. He spent more than an hour of a hot morning stepping in and out of outhouses, making notes on the night soil levels and swatting flies away from his face so that, forty years later, she will read his meticulous thoughts.

She almost believes this. She doesn't understand it – why in the world she's doing this, imagining him this way, but she almost believes it. She smiles to think of him holding his breath, stepping into yet another biffy in a time just before she was born, all for her, somehow.

Sewage and Slop

Except for seven houses in which modern sewage removal systems have been installed, and appear to be pumping satisfactorily, all the private dwellings in the Village continue to employ pit privies. My one concern with these privies, during a routine inspection, is in regard to night soil levels. When they reach approximately 4 feet from the surface, these nearly full pits become a dangerous source of fly breeding.

Dr. Tolley is taking his lunch late. Yes, he's there, at the table, with his chicken sandwich and his crumpled report. He is the only person eating in the hotel, having just inspected the kitchen. The hotel owners knew he'd be coming sometime during the month as did the owners of the other premises he plans to inspect. He wanted to start by being strict but fair. He believes it's in the interest of everyone to provoke higher standards before he arrives rather than to make surprise visits and uncover poor conditions. He thinks about things like this even though he's only begun this job.

He underlines the word Hotel for his next heading and looks over his shoulder to be sure what he writes can't be seen by another. He is inclined to rate the hotel more highly than it deserves because he has become acquainted with the man and his wife who run it, but he can't know exactly what he will say until he writes it. He's learned that in writing, one thing can lead to another and that he might surprise himself, leaping from toilets to sinks to refrigerators, with an opinion he doesn't know he holds. In this way writing is like diagnosis. He was becoming a good diagnostician when he quit his medical practice; he was finding that by emptying his mind and letting his senses and intuition carry him, one thing invariably led to another. Unfortunately the end result was only briefly satisfying. What he won by successful diagnosis he often lost for lack of a cure.

She likes him so much, the young adulteress. Isn't that worth something?

Hotel

There is one hotel in the Village. Its sixteen rooms are of such small proportions (8'x10') that they are not suitable for double occupancy. I am assured that they are usually required by single guests. The bedrooms are adequately furnished and appear to be regularly cleaned. I am of the opinion that the comfort of guests could be increased by the installation of louvred ventilation above each door.

Dr. Tolley is of the private opinion that more than louvred ventilation will be required if he is going to get to sleep tonight. The upstairs rooms have already reached a temperature close to a hundred degrees. However, it's not the hotel's fault he's arrived in a heat wave. Dr.

Tolley takes his handkerchief out of his breast pocket and wipes his face. Sweat is unbecoming to a member of the medical profession and this poses a problem because he feels he must wear a suit in the field and should remove his jacket only in his own room, whatever the consequences to his personal comfort.

The cook, who is co-owner of the hotel with her husband, comes out of the kitchen to clear his table. He slides his elbow across his report and declines her offer of lemonade. He says he might drop in later for a cold drink.

The cook is a tall woman with a slouch that gives her more of a stomach than she should have for her weight. She stands close to him with her hands clasped over her protruding apron. He notices that her hands are red and rough and very clean and commends her on them.

"I just made pastry," she says. "It's always good for cleaning your fingernails."

He can't tell if she's teasing him. Her face is deadpan. He slips the pages of his report into his briefcase and excuses himself.

When he is outside walking down the one cement sidewalk, with the sun high overhead and no more than inches of shade anywhere, the heat sizzles on his skin. It feels hot enough to scorch the fabric of his suit. A wash of sweat cascades from his back and chest and collects at his waistband. Within seconds his waistband is soaked and his belt slides up and down, chafing his middle. He ducks into the Red and White store. The difference in light blinds him momentarily. He sighs as the impression of coolness almost like a breeze floats over him.

"Everybody does that when they come in today," the store owner says. He is just like everybody else, Dr. Tolley, just like any man doing his job the best he can. This morning, after the outhouses, he went with the mayor to visit the well, the village rest rooms, the nuisance ground and the cemetery. On his list for the afternoon are the two general stores, the restaurant, the meat market, the hairdresser's, the hospital, and the dairy, then he must meet with the local medical practitioner. Up and down Main Street he will walk on the shady side, once it develops, and he will smile into the heat, his only obstacle. He mops his face good-naturedly now, in the Red and White store, and grins. He is just like everybody else.

At the end of the afternoon, he hasn't quite accomplished all he set out to do. He decides to put off the dairy for the morning on his way out of town. This makes him a little early for his meeting with the town's only doctor, but he thinks that's preferable to being late. As he stands in the vestibule before the doctor's office, he mops his face for the hundredth time. His grin is weary, not much more than practice. He does not like Bob Berriman. Nevertheless, he's accepted his invitation to take supper with him.

People tend to accept Dr. Berriman's invitations. The adulteress, sitting in the quiet room full of tables and windows, remembers this without knowing how she remembers.

They had planned to meet later, at the Chinese restaurant, but Dr. Tolley is dropping in to see if his colleague will join him for a drink first at the hotel. He thinks a few ounces of whiskey will make supper bearable.

The vestibule is tiny and panelled with dark wood. Stairs to the second floor face the outside entrance. To Dr. Tolley's right is the office door, closed because office hours are over. A square of wavy glass in the top of the door lets a faint shadowy light pass either way but doesn't allow him to see inside. He opens the door.

Directly in front of him a young woman is scrubbing the board floor on her hands and knees. She is wearing short shorts and a white cotton brassiere. He sees her from the side. He sees the tan and white wings of her breasts folded into the brassiere, and her raised, startled face. She has stopped her scrubbing and looked up, but not at Dr. Tolley. She has raised her eyes to Dr. Berriman, who leans against the receptionist's desk with his feet stretched before him, watching her. This tableau lasts only a second or two, then Bob Berriman, his face angry and red, crosses the room with his hand outstretched. He stands in front of the kneeling woman and shakes Dr. Tolley's hand. His footprints remain on the wet floorboards.

"Ready early, are we?" he says. He scoops his jacket off a hook, takes Dr. Tolley's elbow, and steers him out of the office. Dr. Tolley has no opportunity for a second look. A second look isn't necessary.

Bob Berriman asks questions on the way to the hotel, questions about Dr. Tolley's day which Dr. Tolley answers. But not exactly as if nothing has happened. They drink their doubles at the hotel bar in silence. In the Chinese restaurant, where the service is quick, they discuss mutual acquaintances and Dr. Tolley's wife (briefly, Dr. Tolley doesn't like her name on Berriman's lips), and then the possibility of the townspeople adopting septic tanks in place of outhouses. They stretch the meal out with coffee until just after eight when their unexpressed mutual dislike overcomes the conversation and they part. With a long, bright evening before him and his hotel room unbearably hot, Dr. Tolley takes his briefcase to the bar and makes himself busy.

He begins to write about the meat market. He writes that the chopping block was sweet and clean, that the display cases looked as if they had been scoured, that the standard of storage for both implements and meat was high. His pen skims the paper, describing the seemly and professional methods of the butcher in the operation of his shop.

He reports that conditions at the hairdresser in the village were found to be unsatisfactory.

...but it is to be hoped that what I discovered did not represent the usual custom. Neither formalin nor dettol were utilized for sterilizing scissors or combs and one must protest the practice of draping the same rather grimy cape over each unwary client.

Next Dr. Tolley reports on the horrors of the pool hall toilet and the potentially risky practice of discarding hospital garbage in flimsy, insecure containers. And when he has finished that, he caps his pen and puts it down. It comes to him that maybe he has been putting too black an interpretation on the tableau he witnessed in Dr. Berriman's office. Maybe the young woman removed her top in order to be cooler while she worked, not realizing that Berriman was still in the inner office, and Berriman came out and surprised her. Maybe she got up to put her top back on and Berriman said not to bother, she was as decently covered as she would have been at the beach and after all he was a doctor. Maybe she was a casual young woman and agreed. Maybe the fear he thought he felt in the room was his own fear.

Dr. Tolley packs up his papers and takes himself to his room, away from the eyes of two old men who have been drinking coffee in the corner all evening, who have just switched to beer. His room is stifling; it is not possible to remain there.

The thermometer nailed to the hotel wall by the front door says eighty. He contemplated going out in his shirt sleeves, yet he is still dressed in his suit. Even though it's nearly midnight. He could meet someone. It's not for himself he wants to look respectable but for the office.

He strolls up and down the streets and alleys of the village, the same streets and alleys he travelled this morning. They look different in the dark but he hardly notices them; he might be anywhere.

The entire town can be walked in half an hour. In half an hour he turns up Main Street and heads for the hotel. An unexpected sound causes him to notice his surroundings. The sound is of a door opening. He is outside Berriman's office building. He watches as the door swings slowly back against the stucco and a figure steps out into the darkness. It is the young office cleaner. She is completely naked. He thinks that: completely naked. While he watches her walk toward him, he understands: it is a state that can be complete.

She is sleepwalking. Her eyes are open but unseeing. He backs out of her way. She passes close to him (smells of warm bedclothes) and turns to walk down the sidewalk. He follows her.

Now he sees everything in sharp focus, as in a dream. He sees the pock marks in the cement sidewalk and the pebbles in front of her feet, where her feet will land. He hears the soft pad of her bare soles on the cement. On the soles of his own feet, through his shoes, he believes he can feel the coolness and graininess of the cement surface, just as she feels it on her skin.

She passes under the street lamp on the corner. Her dark hair is for a second back lit then the light falls on her shoulders, on the curve of her buttocks and down her calves. She wears a paleness on her torso, like a transparent bathing suit. She walks easily and he walks behind her and the false fronts and cluttered signs and dusty windows of Kerrody roll past them and fall away.

There's only the gleam of the gravel road and the similar faint gleam of her skin. She walks. He follows. A beautiful quiet prevails. He's never been out in the night before, like this. He exhales; it's possible he's been holding his breath since leaving the town. With his breathing resumed, he starts to hear his brogues crunching down, scattering small stones, and the chirping of frogs, loud and exuberant as birds' singing. A splash. So they are near the slough, about a mile from town.

She stops, then turns and walks into the ditch.

Dr. Tolley thinks: she will walk into the slough and drown herself. Then the absurdity of the situation strikes him. He has been following her as if part of her dream, as if a spectator in her dream, with no volition of his own – or as if the dream were his own, as if he had dreamed her and could only watch to see how his dream would end – while in fact he is a responsible medical doctor, a respectable married man, following a naked woman down a country road. Why hasn't he woken her gently, covered her decently and taken her home?

At the edge of the slough is a large rock where that morning, driving into the town, he saw two children fishing. She has climbed up onto that rock. He can just see her pale skin, the slip of water, dark shapes and the sky which, he suddenly notices, is crammed with stars. He has never seen so many stars, near and far, layers and layers of them from the brilliant to the distant almost unseeable. Just for a second he forgets who he is. Then is embarrassed for himself. How easily an atmosphere can fool a man into thinking nothing matters.

She is awake now, she has stepped down from the rock. She is climbing to the road from the ditch and hasn't yet seen him, and then sees him. The sound she makes is a whimper. His body responds with something like pity – a similar fear. Then he remembers who he is.

"I'm Dr. Tolley, the Regional Health Inspector," he says. They look into one another's faces. They both laugh. They laugh harder. It is so absurd, who he is. He takes off his suit jacket and hands it to her. They walk back to town silently. Dr. Tolley allows himself to think of her breasts and belly and buttocks inside his suit jacket.

The door opens as they walk up the path to Berriman's office building. The young woman's husband stands in the vestibule watching them. Before they reach him, he turns and walks up the stairs, which are lit by a bare bulb above the landing. The young woman follows her husband and Dr. Tolley follows her up into a suite of rooms.

"Excuse us," the young man says politely to Dr. Tolley. He leads his wife into their bedroom, closing the door behind them. A few seconds later he emerges with Dr. Tolley's suit jacket.

"Thank you," he says as he hands the jacket to Dr. Tolley. Dr. Tolley drapes it over his arm. The young man stands marooned in the centre of the room. Dr. Tolley could introduce himself, which might be reassuring. He could talk in a clinical way about sleepwalking. He could explain how he'd happened on her. But it all seems superfluous. Without a word he walks out of the room and leaves the young couple behind.

In the morning he drinks a pot of coffee. He sits at his table in the hotel with his head in his hands. The couple who run the hotel speculate, in the kitchen, about what kind of night he had and how long he'll last in this job. He knows they'll be talking about him and doesn't care. All night he lay semi-conscious in a heat-drugged fugue.

He skips the dairy. No, he's much too conscientious to do that. He drives out and drags himself around the milk house, sniffing at the cans, bottles, filters, cooler, and milker, and then he drags himself around the stable and the yard. He is so grateful for the dairy's cleanliness and the remarkable absence of flies that he will give it his most glowing commendation.

Before he turns onto the highway to head home, Dr. Tolley stops to remove his suit jacket. Another hot day is predicted and he can be forgiven, he thinks, for driving in his shirt sleeves in the privacy of his own car. He stops the car at the intersection and steps out to take his jacket off. Just for a second he appreciates the benevolent sky, his solitude. As is his usual practice, he folds the jacket with the lining facing outwards. When he gets into the car, he places the jacket on the passenger seat beside him and starts in third and stalls. That is the last time he will betray himself.

In the room of many tables and windows, the adulteress tries to remember the real story of the town in which she was born. She was very young when they moved away and has little memory of the 119 houses and the small businesses mentioned in the medical health officer's report. Her only vivid memory isn't even her own, it comes from a time before she was born, the memory of a story she heard many times of a short spell in her mother's life when her mother sleepwalked. The high point of the story is the time her mother escaped naked into the night. In the story, the adulteress's father discovered her mother was missing and hauled himself out of bed, pulled on his pants and a shirt, and followed her down Main Street. It was the adulteress's father who brought her mother home. Order was restored and anyone who was told the story laughed to think her mother – her shy young mother of all people – had walked naked through the dark streets where anyone might have seen her.

There is another memory that didn't get made into a story, a more shadowy memory that had to do with the doctor who owned the building they lived in, who had his office on the ground floor. The adulteress's mother cleaned the office for him in exchange for some money off the rent. But that was in a different time and place and the memory is too shadowy to get hold of.

She slips the report into its folder. She is thinking about her mother opening the door, stepping out. She thinks: I've inherited my mother's body. Forgetting where she is, she lifts her arms and stretches – her body is tired from sitting so long perusing those few pages. Across the room, a man looks up.

The Man Who Followed His Hand

About the time the guests were saying it was the nicest part of the evening, the man arrived at Sandra's back yard. The guests were sitting in a circle of chairs on the lawn. They were looking up past the branches of the elms to the sky, where a pink tint informed them that the sun was low. The man stepped into the shade at the corner of the house and waited. Children were playing. He listened to them calling to one another as if great distances separated them. He saw their freckles and flushed cheeks and the sunburnt rims of their ears. He thought: on a summer evening when the last light runs like a river through the suburbs, the voices of children sound lonely.

The children stopped their game when they saw him. The adults gradually noticed the quiet and looked over. Just then Sandra walked out of the house onto the deck.

The man knew nothing about her. He didn't know her name. She was simply a woman he'd followed home the day before, an easy enough accomplishment although she'd been in her car and he'd been on foot. She'd had to drive slowly through the neighbourhood because of the children playing on the streets. A couple of times she'd stopped while they'd pulled their goalie nets aside or wobbled ahead of her on their bikes. He'd seen her eyes through the windshield while she waited at a stop sign longer than she needed to wait because she was watching him walk down the sidewalk. He always knew when people were watching. She turned and looked again when she passed him. Funny how people didn't realize they could be seen through car windows. He'd often wondered at it. He didn't drive, himself. He didn't follow women to their homes either, usually.

She hugged a salad bowl to her chest, breathing in the smell of garlic. At first she didn't see him. She thought the guests were looking at her and wondering when they'd get to eat. She hadn't been ready when they'd arrived. She'd forgotten to put the wine into the fridge and to take the steaks out. Her hair was still wet from the shower. David was just beginning to nudge the children's leftover hot dogs to the back of the barbecue grills and slide the steaks on, having no doubt waited for her to appear with the salad. This is why we have these parties, she thought. The women toss the salads. The men tend the barbecues. Three men were standing ready to help her husband prod the steaks, they all had beers in their hands. David knew how to make the others feel at home. She used to know how, but it seemed she had lost the knack. She had already offended the women by refusing to allow them into her kitchen. She hadn't offended her neighbour from across the street, though, to be fair. Nothing much bothered her beautiful, bleached-blonde neighbour. Without so much as a hello, Emily had set a tray of brownies from Safeway on the picnic table and made her way cheerfully to the cooler for a beer. An admirable woman, a good-natured soul, with no great affinity for kitchens.

Sandra had chased the other women from her house. She'd given them carrot sticks and potato chips and empty hot dog buns and sent them to feed their children. She'd been rude to Lou, her husband's boss's wife, who'd tried to make her write down the recipe for her vegetable appetizer pizza. But Lou was already drunk by then, so it really hadn't mattered.

One of the men at the barbecues called to the man in the shade by the corner of the house. "Grab a lawn chair," he said, "and come on over." Harvey was one of the older men who had lived in the subdivision for years, which meant that he could take over the host's role when the host was busy, in this case telling a joke, one all of them swore they hadn't heard. The man didn't respond to Harvey's invitation. He stood staring at them. The other guests smiled and shifted their chairs, repeating the welcome.

How relaxed they looked – in their perfect, convivial circle. How sure of themselves and each other and the occasion. Light and shadows floated over them as if the setting sun and a playful breeze conspired in their perfection. The man knew it was an illusion, that perfection, harmony, accord. And he knew this was the difference between himself and them: they, being involved, were unconscious of the illusion they created and tried to maintain, while he, the intruder, was all too conscious of his desire to join them. Yet he hesitated, prolonging the moment of their perfection, knowing his joining them would destroy it.

Sandra was not impressed by her guests. She thought their benevolence was easy. She was not in the mood to give them credit. She had been tired of them, without knowing why, before she'd even begun with them, tired of their golf games and their house renovations and the many accomplishments of their ever-active offspring. Tired of their sociability.

She recognized the man, of course. He remained by the corner of the house, refusing the others' invitation. He gazed at them, seriously; he seemed to her to be estimating their good will, taking the temperature of the party. His right arm was a little raised, his hand tentatively forward. The children stared at him. The adults looked embarrassed.

"What a lovely yard," they'd said when they'd arrived, the ones who hadn't visited before. "Your trees are huge," they'd said. "Isn't it nice to sit out here under the trees on an evening like this." Sandra had always thought of herself as a woman who had no conversation, but perhaps none was better than this. Every time someone new had arrived, the others had nodded and looked up into these trees, which were nothing but straggly American elms, as if they'd been given to them to sit under, as if something depended on the scrawny branches bobbing in the breeze. This is what we share, they seemed to be telling one another, the shade, the breeze, the trembling leaves. David understood. He wanted them to be happy. He offered them wine and beer as soon as they sat down.

Many of the guests didn't know one another, even some of those who were neighbours hadn't met, but they were all used to meeting strangers. David had made the introductions. "I don't think you know everyone," was his standard line. One of the women said, "No, but how nice to see new faces." These words buzzed in Sandra's mind over and over, whenever her husband introduced someone new.

"How nice to see new faces," she whispered, hugging her salad bowl, standing on the deck above them. They all knew so well what was expected of them, but they didn't know what to do about the man standing in the shade of the house with his hand outstretched.

He'd been walking down the sidewalk in a very distinctive way. She had seen him before she'd pulled up beside him. Then she'd stayed at the stop sign longer than she needed to, watching him. She hadn't meant to stare. At the time, she was almost sure he didn't notice her, he was so involved with making his way down the sidewalk, following his erratic hand. And he did follow his hand, she saw that immediately. Wherever his hand pointed, his body was pulled. The intriguing thing was that he'd devised a way of directing his course. With his free hand, the one he could control, he guided, from time to time, the hand that led him. So he made his way, slowly and awkwardly, but effectively. She admired him greatly. She felt as if the rest of the world had fallen away. Only he remained. He might have been the last man on earth, that's how alone he was on that sidewalk, dependent only on himself, his one commitment the carving out of his own path. He followed his hand, nothing else, so he could survive, she told herself, when all around him had perished.

Except for the odd bird's chatter, the yard was quiet. The only movement was in the trees. The branches swayed. Slanting light caught the undersides of the leaves and Sandra imagined the yard submerged in water. In the time between the birds' calls and the sighing of the branches she heard an underwater sound. She saw that the guests had become tense and David was deciding what he should do. He was holding a barbecue fork uselessly in both hands. Soon he would have to put it down and do something.

"Where's Jack?" Sandra asked him, before he could make a move. She knew that the dog was tied at the side of the house where he couldn't see strangers and bark at them. David didn't bother to look up. After eighteen years of marriage, he didn't answer questions she asked for her own purposes. He knew what to ignore. But their son Jamie was sitting on the grass below the deck and heard his mother.

He didn't like the silence between his parents. He didn't want them to embarrass him. Now that he was twelve, he often found he hated adults and their ways, especially the silences that meant so much. He answered his mother's question.

Sandra felt ashamed, looking at her son. At least for him, she should be sociable. She should help David get rid of the strange man and make their invited guests feel comfortable again. She looked very seriously at Jamie to focus her better intentions. His face was getting longer, the bones more prominent. He was not a little boy; he would never again sit on her knee. She wasn't a particularly wise mother. She'd have detained him if she could have thought of a way to keep him by her side. She would have run her hand over his hair, but he took off as she reached out.

Before David could decide what to do about the situation, the man advanced into the yard, hand first. He walked between the children and their parents. A few of the parents stood up. One of the smallest boys jumped to his feet and ran blindly toward the adults. The man showed no inclination to stop, if he noticed the boy at all. He was so intent, it was doubtful he saw anything but the circle of lawn chairs which was where he seemed to be headed. The little boy cut through his path. They nearly collided. When he got to the circle, the child searched out his mother and burrowed his head into her lap.

Sandra set the salad bowl on the deck and took hold of the railing. The man continued in his way and she watched him, once again fascinated by his ability to single-mindedly pursue his own path. A few times he was pulled off course when his arm swung outward at a right angle to his body. With a jerk each time, his body followed and he struck off toward the side yard. When that happened, he took his left hand and deliberately, sharply slapped at his right until he was back on course. In this way he reeled toward the guests who could do nothing but watch while their host, at last doing something, tried to intercept him.

Twice David nearly caught him but the man veered off. Leaving David stranded. Leaving him facing Sandra, feeling that his face and neck had turned red. He thought he knew what she was thinking. She was thinking he deserved this fuss. Because it was his idea to have the party. He was sure she telegraphed this information to him, standing calmly erect above him, her hands resting lightly on the railing. For an instant he wanted to kill her.

She saw it in his face. It was the most hopeful thing she'd seen in months.

With the exception of Lou, the boss's wife, who was much too loaded to care, and Emily, the beautiful bleached-blonde neighbour, who liked a good fight, the guests were embarrassed. The host and hostess were behaving badly. And they were doing nothing to stop the man who was working his way toward them, diligently prodding his right hand, with every step following its direction.

When the man finally reached the circle, Harvey, the neighbour who'd invited him to join them, stood up and said, "Hey, hey now." Several of the guests stood and stepped back from their chairs. David strode over, grabbed the man's arm and swung him around.

Some of the guests looked as though they were afraid of a fight, but the man himself was not surprised by David's anger. He was doing what he thought Sandra wanted, invading the party. It was only right that her husband would be upset.

Sandra wished the man would say something to the guests, something no one else could tell them. They would have to believe such an artless man. But then she chided herself; it was she who should change rather than trying to change everyone else. She was always wanting people to be more than they could be.

"What can we do for you?" David was asking the man. He might have been talking to any one of the guests, he accorded the man that much dignity. He spoke quietly, his anger gone.

Sandra loved her husband. He didn't ask anything of anyone that he wouldn't expect of himself. She tried to hold that moment, when he forgot her and the guests and himself, and cared only about this man.

While she was telling herself she wouldn't forget it, would keep it separate somehow in her mind for future use, the moment was being transmuted by what happened next. Jamie had slipped around the house to the side yard and untied the dog. He was afraid of the strange man, unsure of his father's gentle methods and he thought the dog would strengthen David's authority over their yard. Jack bounded up barking just because he was free. He leapt into the circle and lunged for his master's legs. He frightened the stranger. The man stood paralyzed.

"Get down," David yelled. He yelled at Jamie too. "Tie Jack up," he ordered. "Get him out of here and tie him up."

The man was shaking. He didn't know what to do next, where to go. The guests, too, didn't know what might be expected of them.

Jamie took the dog away. Sandra saw his face, the knowledge that he'd done the wrong thing. His long face, with the changing bones.

They would all be bones one day, she thought, watching Jamie then David, the man and their guests. In her mind, she stepped away from them while the discussion about the man went on without her. Again she imagined the yard submerged in water, and she thought of their bones floating along the grass like the leaves floating on the breeze. They would all be bones one day so the square footage of their houses and the scores of the golf games and the trophies their children brought home should not matter to them. They should concern themselves with bigger things. It was wrong to judge them on their dinner party conversation, but she was sick of never hearing anything else. She would rather be alone than be with them.

She remembered finding herself alone in a room filled with Henry Moore sculptures, once, in the provincial art gallery in Toronto. The strange, sad forms surrounded her. They reminded her of human bones, of human dinosaurs. Among them, she felt she was mourning. Yet she could see they were the bones of people who had been strong and good and had for a time endured. They were huge and their largeness made her bigger. And now she stood in the midst of a party in her own back yard, hating everyone in sight.

They were all talking, suddenly they all had something to say. One of the women was sure she'd seen the man before, in the library downtown, where the derelicts hang out when it's too hot or too cold outside. Nobody would admit to thinking he was dangerous, but a few of them went so far as to say they were uneasy in his presence. He stood in the centre of the circle with David, and the guests talked about him as if he wasn't there. He seemed to be staring at nothing, but Sandra thought he heard them. She came down from the deck and joined her husband and the man. "How about some supper?" she asked them both. David ignored her and asked the man, again, "What can we do for you?" The man peered up into the trees as if the answer might be there. Someone suggested they call the police to come and pick him up.

"Nonsense," Sandra said. "Aren't you all hungry? I'm starved." She looked over to the barbecues where Wayne, their next door neighbour, still stood guard. "I guess the steaks will be well done," she said.

"About medium right now, if you get a move on," Wayne said.

The man understood that he was still needed at the party, but he had been frightened by the dog and he didn't know what he should do next. He waited for a sign.

Sandra ushered the guests over to the picnic table where the plates were piled. Some of them dragged their feet a bit, but they were hungry, they soon followed the others. Sandra asked Jamie to bring over the salad and to get a ball or something new for the other children to play with. He gave her a look that said her behaviour was only barely acceptable and wouldn't much longer be tolerated. Even so, she asked the children what they would like to do next as she walked toward them, her arms flapping as if she was shooing chickens. They were about as dear to her right then as a flock of chickens in her yard. What they wanted to do, of course, at least the older ones, was watch to see what would happen next between the adults and this strange man. When Jamie came down with the salad, she insisted that he take the children to the front of the garage where they could shoot baskets. He said it was getting too dark to shoot baskets. He glared at her, but she wouldn't respond, so he turned and followed her bidding, and the others reluctantly followed him.

Next she advanced on the adults. "Eat, eat," she ordered the few who were still without plates. "Here's the salad," she called to the others. She took a plate over to the man who was still standing beside David, gazing into the trees. "What would you like?" she asked him. "Would you like a steak? Some salad?" She took his arm and began to lead him to the barbecues. David stared after her; she felt his disgust on her back. With no warning, the man pulled away and began walking very quickly about the yard. He didn't bump into anyone, but he came close a few times. "He's marching," someone said as he strode by, his arm held high like a drum major, his head high too, his feet lifting high off the ground and coming smartly down. "He's marching, all right," someone else said quietly.

The yard was getting darker; the sun was almost set. David was deciding to call the police. Sandra was deciding she wouldn't let him.

She blocked his way onto the deck, knowing he wouldn't want to risk a confrontation. "I'll put on some more music," she said. "Something quiet. He'll calm down." Because she knew her husband deserved more, she added that she couldn't bear to think of the man being taken away. Then she got back to her hostess duties, completely forgetting the music. She interrupted two women who were talking about taking their children home. "Come on," she said, linking her arms into theirs and steering them back to the lawn chairs. "This is supposed to be a party. Where are your glasses? I'll get some more wine."

On her way back with the wine bottle, she dragged a few more people into the circle. "Relax," she told them. Then music tripped out across the yard and Sandra stopped short. The guests looked at one another. It was Beethoven's Sixth, the Pastoral Symphony. Visions of court ladies, in peasant dress, danced on the lawn.

"What is this?" someone asked. They all listened.

Sandra said, "I think it's the sound of my husband mocking me."

Some of the guests giggled nervously. The music was so out of place and yet so apt, or perhaps it was the time that was wrong and the place that was so right. The man who followed his hand loved it. He adapted immediately. He danced over the grass among the trees. His spirits rose as the music rose. Sandra had a silly wish that she could join him, that all of them could rise up off their cheap plastic lawn chairs and dance in the twilight under the trees, sway with the music – and cry. She would have liked to cry while she danced.

A little girl was standing where the man first appeared at the corner of the house. She was crying. Sandra saw her and went to her. She knelt beside her. "I feel like you," she said. This information did nothing to soothe the child, who sobbed all the harder. Her father came along and asked what was wrong. She said she wanted to go home. "No, no," Sandra said. "Don't go. It's all right to cry." The child's father beckoned to the mother and before Sandra could rise to her feet, they were leaving. "The music's too loud," she said to herself, but she did nothing to change it.

The man who followed his hand stopped under the tree nearest to the circle of lawn chairs, his arm upraised, his eyes again on the leaves as they fluttered and floated. "Don't go," Sandra said, seeing another couple get to their feet. "Please," she said, and they sat again. "Have some more wine," she said. "It's a party. It's early." David came over with two plates, loaded. He handed one to her and kept the other for himself. They sat on opposite sides of the circle. "I'm starving," she said, digging in.

The music began to storm. Even when it was quiet, it held the threat of more storm. The sky was suddenly as dark as it would get all night. The man followed his hand up the tree. He climbed as high as he could and sat huddled against the trunk, pointing down at the guests. The music punched at them, then fondled them, over and over, alternately, and all the time the man in the tree pointed at them and Sandra wanted to cry hard and David ignored everything and all the guests wanted to leave. The music seemed to know more than they did about their own lives and they found it unbearable to sit under such knowledge, such insistent, repetitive knowledge of themselves and the more tender the music got, the harder it was for them to listen and finally they just all got up and left. Neither the host nor the hostess bothered to say goodbye.

They sat across from one another, full of the music and things unsaid. Better left unsaid, in David's opinion. But Sandra's thoughts lifted and fell with the music. All our bones are fragile, she wanted to say, all our thoughts are weak, our passions puny, and our souls scrabble on the ground in the dust and dead leaves. Or we are too light, we rise too easily to the surface. We should be heavier, stronger. We should work harder, climb steadily, and not look back.

David rose to his feet and began to gather the plates and napkins and empty beer bottles. We should have passions, Sandra was thinking. We should dare something, risk something, strive for something. We should try to be bigger than we are. We should want to leave something behind for others to see. None of her thoughts stopped him from his cleaning up. Back and forth he went, from the yard to the house, carting food and garbage, and she raged because everyone had left, they'd followed one another and left because they were people who wanted only to follow one another. They had no passion, no greatness, no anger or real love. They wanted only to do what the others did and not be embarrassed, not be revealed for what they were. They wanted to live their lives undisturbed by strangers. They wanted to meet only the strangers who could not disturb, only those who were not really strangers at all because they were just like them, more followers after the same followers. So they had gone. And she was left with her husband, who cleaned up the mess in silence.

She was angry about the silence too, because the music had died too soon and not strongly enough for her. There was too much village festival and shepherd's song and not enough storm. How could she say to David while he hosed down the barbecues, making the coals hiss and steam, that she hated his cleaning up, that she wanted to fight. He knew she wanted to fight, he'd known it all evening, and he wasn't going to let her. Please, she would have said to him if there were any way of saying it, please just let's fight. Their son had gone to bed or at least he'd gone to his room or to watch TV. Only the man in the tree would hear them and he wouldn't care. It was time to quit being host, she wanted to tell her husband. It was time to stand up and fight. He pulled the lids down over the barbecues and turned to face her. She couldn't say a thing.

He pitied her for a moment. Then he left her.

She watched him walk steadily across the lawn and up the steps to the house and she knew he wasn't going to change his mind. She turned her chair to face the tree where the man still huddled although she could no longer see him for the darkness, and his hand no longer pointed at anyone. Now that David was gone, she tried to remember the moment when he was good to the man, that moment she'd remembered she loved him. But she couldn't really imagine it. She kept thinking, instead, of him walking away from her and both of them knowing he wasn't going to turn around. Both of them knowing the door would not open, he would not come down those steps, he wasn't going to fight or even talk. Over and over again, her memory took him across the lawn, up the steps, away from her.

All night the man waited in the tree, thinking he'd been forgotten.

When the light came up in the morning, she heard a movement in the branches. A hand reached down hesitantly, as if testing the water. It was a frail, thin hand, the skin almost translucent in the rosy light. Inside it, the bones trembled.

The Frogs in Early Summer

Megan is reading a book about someone reading a book. She is so far into the story she almost has the feeling she is reading the book the other woman is reading, and inhabiting the other woman's world. Her own world consists at this time of her apartment balcony and the balconies, windows, and rooftops she can see from the twelfth floor. And a patch of smoggy sky. She is sitting on her one canvas sling chair with her feet on the balcony railing. But she is not really aware of her surroundings. She is reaching for something – in the book or in herself. The story she is reading and the story within the story are giving her the feeling that there is something she has lost, that there is something she had her hands on once that has slipped away.

A boy (not in either story in her book) says, "I'll show you something on the other side." He speaks clearly to her in her imagination. He is as present as he can be, although not of course on the balcony beside her. They are sitting on the edge of the dugout on his father's farm. His father's farm is entirely present. It is evening, after the supper hour. His parents are in the farmhouse. She believes her parents are there too, visiting with his. She is sitting on the grass at the edge of the dugout, beside the boy, as young as he is. Her legs dangle over the water beside his. A chill rises from the brown water and the bank is damp so in spite of the warm breeze, their bodies are in pre-shiver state.

She knows who he is. No memory of hers. No boy she could have had her hands on. He is Hertha's boy. She is delighted to find him and to be so sure of who he is. She has often wondered about him; now he has come to her. She supposes he has come because she is in this nostalgic state of mind. And because she is either too young or too much of her time to feel nostalgia for her own life. And because romance belongs to the past, and to ruined women, like Hertha.

The boy says, "I'll show you a secret on the other side." Sitting beside her, he is inches taller than she is. His eyes are focussed on the other side. The night is beginning to fall across the prairie in long shadows as if the light has split to let the darkness in. He is already on the other side, in spirit, and restless, even there.

"Can we swim across?" she asks. It's not far, after all, maybe thirty feet. The other side is metaphorical, not impossible.

"They'd kill us," he says. Which makes them conspirators against their parents. He is smiling across the dugout. Silently their phantom bodies slide over the edge. Their toes hit the cold water. With a kick of their heels at the muddy wall, they propel themselves, arms steepled, to the other side. But there is no getting out because they have not quite got in.

"We'll have to walk around," she says and two thoughts come to her before she has finished her sentence. One is the thought of the cool damp fine new grass and the wiry soft prairie wool alternating under her bare feet. The other is the thought that he will kiss her as soon as he can.

But she is in her chair on her balcony with the sunlight bouncing off the open pages of her book. She can't stay long enough on the slippery bank of the dugout for the boy to kiss her.

He remembers he was shy as a boy. He remembers how many times he wanted to kiss a girl, how many girls, and how seldom he did. All the girls he might have kissed. He remembers Hertha.

When Megan remembers Hertha, she thinks of The Club. A stage in her life, that's all The Club is now, as in: public school, high school, The Club. And when she thinks of it, she seems to be remembering something much further in the past than the actual passage of years would justify. Maybe that's because The Club doesn't exist anymore.

She drove by the day after the fire, in traffic like a funeral procession. People inching past, circling the block to get a second look at a building with its insides hollowed out and its skeleton dripping icicles two feet thick and twelve feet long, bubbled stacked icicles and glass-clear icicle sheets. The Club was a cold, glassy beauty, a castle of ice, floating above the street, prism-like, breaking the light into colours, with exhaust wafting over it and the frosty sun and a pair of sun dogs shining through. People who'd never been to The Club took pictures. It didn't matter to them what the building had been, they were responding to the beauty it presented for as long as the cold spell continued.

Megan used to go to The Club with a group of friends. She had money in those days, the two years after high school that she worked. She was working to save for a trip to Europe and the Middle East with a friend of hers. But the friend got married instead and Megan didn't feel like making the trip alone. She felt alone enough when she was around people she knew, so she decided to go to school instead.

A new Club started up in a strip mall after the old one burnt down, but nobody Megan knows goes there. The people Megan knows don't go anywhere anymore except to school, to their part-time jobs and to bed. If some of them still get together, it isn't in a nightclub in a strip mall that has big flat windows facing a parking lot.

People could find the old Club only if they knew it was there, past the black-painted door in the brick wall and up the unlit, unswept stairs of the old warehouse. People of all ages met there, students, artists, and writers – or people who looked like students, artists, and writers. People tended to wear black and smoke. The owners played French songs, the kind of songs that croon "amour" in every other line, and they encouraged eccentrics. They had one dependable nonconformist, a woman who sat at a table in the corner talking to herself every evening. Hertha.

Megan remembers the night of the frogs best. All the other nights she sat at tables with her friends talking about their futures have been subsumed into that one night that, ironically, focussed on the past. That night – a cold night in November – Hertha was the best the management could do for eccentric. A couple of kids on the other side of the room wore matching Mohawks and black lipstick, the girl had brilliant blue teardrops dribbling down one cheek, but they were trying.

In the centre of the room, that night, were a man and a woman who didn't belong there. The man was dressed in a three-piece suit. He was probably the only person within miles of The Club on that cold night who had a tan. The woman could have stepped from the pages of a Sears catalogue. She was the only woman in the room whose shoes and purse matched. They were drinking beer. People were watching them because they seemed to have forgotten they were sitting in the middle of a room full of people. Hertha was watching them too. She smiled whenever she looked in their direction. Hertha sat in the corner by a window that was lit every other second by a neon sign across the street. Everyone knew Hertha. She came early every night and drank three glasses of red wine and paid for two. The waiters wouldn't let anyone else have her table; they knew she liked looking out. They were worried when the neon was installed across the street, that it would bother her or even set her off into some kind of seizure, but she looked through it or over it or maybe just at the black glass and her own reflection in it.

"What's Hertha talking about tonight?" somebody asked the waiter who'd taken her her second glass of wine. He said she was talking about frogs.

Everyone wanted to know what Hertha had to say about frogs. The waiter shrugged. He said, "Apparently, there were a lot of them."

In the centre of the room, the woman with the matching shoes and purse rested her head on her hand while she listened to the man. Once in a while she nodded or spoke a few words. Everything he said seemed to make her happier. People at Megan's table started inventing stories about them. All the stories ended with the couple leaving holding hands, as if they were young again.

"Look at Hertha," someone at the next table said. Hertha was leaning her head on her hand like the woman in the centre of the room. Once in a while she looked up, smiled and nodded her head, then spoke as if to someone at her table.

"Why does she do that?" one of the women at the next table asked. She sounded embarrassed for Hertha. Nobody answered.

"Go talk to her, Rob," somebody said. "She likes you." But Rob said no. Finally one of the guys, Gerry Anderson, got up and went to stand in the window as if to look out over the city, and tried to pick up on the conversation she was having with herself.

He didn't stay long, but long enough that Hertha shifted in her chair and talked to him. When he returned to the table, he didn't say much. He must have given them some of the details, though, because Megan has them in her mind. She has the night at the dugout in her mind, like one of those quiet pockets of time she has experienced in her own life. The smell of mud comes to her with the picture of Hertha tossing her head and running her fingers through her hair, imitating the woman in the centre of the room. She thinks it was good of Gerry to stand beside Hertha while she talked on and on about the frogs. She sees him standing guard, as in O *Canada*, standing guard for Hertha, for them all. Something in his stance, in the angle of his chin as he looked out, in the set of his shoulders, made them safe.

The boy walks ahead of her, unself-consciously leading the way along a path cows have made around the dugout. He doesn't know his shoulders and his upper back are beautiful to her. She follows him to the other side. There, in the grass on that side, are hundreds of frogs. It is obvious that she and the boy are still half children. They run from the dugout to a tractor tire near a shed, with frogs in their hands. They catch frogs faster and faster because the sun is going down and before long they won't be able to see them. She cups her hands around the tiny frogs. They hop in her hands. Then she releases them into the tire. When she and the boy are tired and they can see only by the yard light, they lean over the tire and try to estimate how many frogs they have. Hundreds.

He remembers worrying that his parents would hear them calling to one another and think it was getting late. He remembers trying to quiet

Hertha, but she was excited by the frogs, and she kept calling to him when she found more. After they'd gathered hundreds, he said they should go back around to the other side of the dugout. The spot he'd picked was the only place where shrubs grew, the only place they couldn't be seen from the house. They sat there at the edge of the dugout and he kissed her. They lay back in the damp grass and kissed.

In the centre of the room, that night at The Club, the woman with the matching shoes and purse started shredding the label on her beer bottle, letting foil curls fall to the table. The man with the tan was looking at his watch.

Hertha's third glass was empty. She had no label to shred. She'd been running her fingers down her glass, watching them. She held her hand up to the waiter when he came to remove her glass. Later, at Megan's table, he repeated what she said. "My hands are old," she said. "Somehow, in the last few years, they've become my mother's hands."

The man in the centre of the room stood up and pulled on his topcoat and the woman looked distressed. Hertha looked sad too. The night, obviously, wasn't going to end in the promising way it had begun. But no one in The Club was expecting violence. When the man stood and the woman remained sitting, looking up at him, everyone thought her charming. With those slightly tired eyes of hers, she was pretty still. When she reached her arm out and laid her hand on the man's, Hertha did the same, in the corner, with the waiter. The waiter didn't hit Hertha, though he might have. She recoiled as if he had. That was likely instinctive. Having put herself in the other woman's place, she felt the blow. A lot of people in the room stood up. Everyone remembered the sound of the man's open hand against the woman's face.

The man walked out of The Club. The woman sat with her head down. People stood, not knowing where to look. The waiter left Hertha's table and went to the woman to ask if there was anything he could do to help. She shook her head. In the corner, Hertha shook hers.

He remembers Hertha's smile. They had been staring at the stars, waiting for a shooting star, and she turned to him and said it didn't matter to her if she never saw a shooting star. Then she smiled. And he remembers thinking he knew what she would look like when she grew up and became a woman.

The next morning they slept in. The sun was high in the sky by the time they came out to look at their frogs in the tractor tire. It was a mistake to try to keep them. They couldn't live without water. She was shocked. She was a city girl. He told her it was nature; they live only a short time.

In the centre of the room, the woman rose from her chair. Everyone watched, pretending not to watch, as she picked up her purse from the floor and held it near her chest. People felt restless, watching her leave, as though something that should have been resolved now never would be.

Hertha got up from her table and wandered toward the exit, pulling her coat on as she walked through the room and muttering to herself.

"How's it going, Hertha?" Rob asked when she passed Megan's table. Rob was the one the others said she liked. She gave him one of her smiles.

He hopes Hertha remembers the night they found the frogs and kissed, he hopes that memory is what comes to mind if she ever thinks of him. He knows that in her twenties she had what were labelled schizophrenic episodes and he has heard from his parents that she isn't doing well. It would be easy to think she was always an odd girl. Or vulnerable. But she was simply herself. The morning they found the dead frogs, she didn't blame him or change toward him or act traumatized. She took his hand and stood with him.

They went out the door together that night, the whole bunch from the table. They walked down the stairs, all laughing and talking at once and turning up their coat collars before stepping out into the cold. There were six of them. They were easy together. Somebody commented you could see your breath so thick you could make smoke rings of it. Megan remembers they tried, but she can't remember if they did it. Then they said goodnight and found their separate ways home.

She ran into Gerry Anderson on the street one day. This was after The Club burnt down. She hadn't seen him in a while; she hadn't seen anybody. They met going in opposite directions at a crosswalk and he walked back with her to her corner. She asked him if he ever saw Hertha and he had seen her, once, at a bus stop, talking to herself.

They stood awkwardly on the street corner, looking as if they were going to move on, although it seemed there was more to say. When he said good-bye, he reached out and touched his finger to the tip of her nose. A good feeling came with that touch, a little jump between them. Then he was gone. She watched him cross the street.

Since Megan stopped reading her book, the earth has moved a few degrees and now the sun shines in her face. She pushes her chair back into the strip of shade cast by the balcony above. In the process, her book falls to the cement. The early summer breeze lifts the pages in slow motion. Bending, she tries to catch words. She sees Elmer, Mrs. Dennehy, Dr. Cormican, Mary Louise, Robert, Aunt Emmeline. All these people who live in this book, people she knows better than any of the hundreds of people who live close to her, in her building, in any of the buildings crowded up to hers. People she knows better than anyone she could really meet, better than anyone could know her. Yet she imagines herself walking into her apartment, setting her book down by the telephone. She sees herself paging through the phone book, another book that must hold stories within stories. She pictures herself dialing Gerry Anderson's number, perhaps calling more than one of the G. Andersons listed in the phone book, until she makes contact with him – because it is important to make contact, to keep contact. Because you have to try.

The Fat Lady with the Thin Face

On her tour of the abbey grounds, Linda comes to the hen house door and finds herself confronted. It's a bit unsettling. First one chicken raises its head and sees her, then another looks up from jabbing the ground, then another. Soon they've all raised their heads with those limp slabs of red flesh wobbling any which way, and they've all stepped toward her. One chicken shrieks, another takes up the cry, then they all open their beaks and berate her. She supposes she shouldn't take it personally; this must be the welcome they give anyone who has nothing to give them.

She has nothing for the pigs either, but they don't care. Although their smell is aggressive, their house is calm. It's divided into pens, each pen dominated by a sow with her litter scattered around her. A few of the piglets watch Linda pass through. Others are sleeping or feeding or stumbling over one another. The sows ignore her. They are huge and confidently insouciant. She almost envies them. If she were more like them, she would not be here, or anywhere alone. She would travel with her husband (now her ex-husband), when she travelled, and a monastery would not be their destination.

On her way back to the guest lodge, she comes to the raspberry patch. She imagines the sun-warmed tang of the berries on her tongue and detours into the patch. She nearly steps on a monk. He is lying on his back in the raspberry patch. He smiles up at her.

"Yoga," he says. "Deep relaxation."

Michele, on her way to visit the pigs, comes to the raspberry patch. It's a hot day and the raspberries smell as strong on the path as they would in the kitchen if her mother were making jam. Michele ambles. She is keeping her eyes open for her favourite monk, Brother Cory, who almost became a rock star. An extremely pretty woman is standing among the raspberries. She has fair hair. She is slender and poised and manages to be still gracefully. Michele's favourite monk, Brother Cory, stands up beside her. For a second, Michele imagines he has been on his knees proposing. The first time she saw him she thought he was too good-looking to waste himself being a monk. Now, while she watches, he throws back his handsome head, laughing at something the pretty woman has murmured. He stands head and shoulders above the canes, with his black hair and his black cowl and his knowledge of everything Michele doesn't know.

She strides past beans and cabbages and onions. She could have known all he knows. By now she would have known, if she hadn't refused the closest thing to an offer she's ever had. She scowls at the rows of vegetables. The pretty woman talks to Brother Cory in the raspberries; if Michele were ever lucky enough to corner him for an intimate chat it would be in the turnips. But then she has one of those flashes from a book that come to her sometimes. This one is of Tess of the d'Urbervilles standing in a frozen field of turnips. Either Hardy put Tess there or Michele did, while reading. At any rate, it seems romantic now. Fists of turnips punishing the ground, she remembers from somewhere. But it isn't turnips she's picturing, it's wheat, flat-topped fields of wheat, summer-green and not yet knee-high.

"Hey Beautiful!" they'd yelled. Beautiful. The gravel road had taken her through farmers' fields; she'd walked until she'd forgotten where she was. They drove up behind her. They were two guys about her age or a little younger, in a truck. "Hey Beautiful!" they yelled. "How about a blow job?" She saw that they were smirking when they slowed down and had no real intention of stopping. "Wanna be our girlfriend?" the driver crooned. She walked alongside the truck and looked them over. A warm friendly wind pushed her from behind. The air smelled of stinkweed, wildly sweet. They were good-looking boys, squinting at her from the cab of their truck. They would have been surprised if she'd said, "Sure."

Hurrying from Vespers to supper, Brother Bernard rehearses his thoughts.

Each day slices open. Just as the Red Sea parted to let the Israelites through, each day slices open three times at the abbey.

He has recently returned after several months of study in the States. Now the abbey seems exotic to him.

And time is suspended and all the activities that keep us busy are suspended while we gather, not at the river but at the dining hall, and file through the food line rather than the miraculous river bed. We give thanks for our food as the Israelites did, no doubt, for their deliverance, and we have our earthly communion, eating together and sharing the events and complaints of the day which perhaps the Israelites dispensed with on that auspicious occasion. Each day and all our happenings are much the same; the provision for our needs is always miraculous when you regard it freshly.

He finds himself next to Michele in line. Oh humbug. He blushes to think she might have read his thoughts, to think that even the tone of his high-flying thoughts might have communicated itself to her, or that a pompous look on his face might have leaked his love of those rollicking syllables. He cannot think of a thing to say to her. Luckily she is scowling at the closed kitchen doors. He cannot think of a thing to think, either, now that he's afraid to think of his phrases, so he waits as he supposes a dog must wait, for six o'clock. But not as a dog waits, no, because a dog doesn't understand time's divisions, its constitution simply responds to its needs. Intriguing idea. He might write a paper comparing a dog with its tongue hanging out to himself standing in line with his tray in his hands.

He is always writing. When he has no pen in his hand, he rehearses lines for papers he might write so he won't forget them. Each line seems precious to him, but he's embarrassed by his habit. It's vain to think such lines would matter to anyone else, matter so much that he must get them down word perfect.

Even when he empties his mind – as he must – Brother Bernard feels the pressure of his thoughts, his vain thoughts dressed in bombast, piling up either side of the small space he's been able to hew, the small quiet space where the voice of God might be heard before the sound of his own voice floods back. He doesn't wait in line at all as a dog would wait. He waits rehearsing. The thoughts sneak back so he hardly notices, then tumble over one another in their eagerness.

At six exactly, as always happens, the doors open, giving us a flash view of the utilitarian kitchen (bare white and dull metal) and the sisters file out and lift the lids off the food that has been waiting, untouchable before this ritual, for the sisters must exert some small control. The sisters step back while the steam rises and the line presses forward eagerly, as if we haven't eaten this day and might not be fed on the morrow. The sisters watch our backs, pretending to find fault with our posture or the dirt on our shoes but really trying not to acknowledge our greed or show their own gratification. Three times a day, our weakness is abundantly visible. Their ability to fill us, to satisfy us, only to see us here again a few hours later with our need in our hands, our plates held out, is cause for celebration among them.

The doors open. The sisters descend on the hot food bins. The steam rises, cumulonimbus.

At times their gloating is audible to us when we return our depleted trays to the kitchen window and catch them remarking how much Father So-and-So ate today and what a fondness Brother So-and-So has for this or that, and how quickly the desserts go; the men like their sweets.

With his tray laden, Brother Bernard follows Michele into the dining room and over to the table where several of the monks have settled into their regular spots. During the other meals this week, Michele has joined them at this table, but tonight Father Gregory, the guestmaster, takes her arm before she can set her tray down. Speaking in a low voice, he walks her across the room to a table where the pretty woman who arrived this afternoon is sitting alone. She and Michele are the only individual retreatants at the abbey. The other guests who occupy a third table are part of a group retreat studying spiritual graphology with Father Morris Abernathy, a noted Catholic graphologist from California. Michele does not look pleased to have been ousted from the monks' table and asked to sit with the pretty woman.

Brother Bernard digs into his meal without tasting anything, not even the tomatoes the guests always rave about that don't taste anything like the ones you buy in the grocery stores. He tries to visualize Michele without looking at her. Then he tries to find words to fit the shape she takes in his mind.

A roundness of cheek and eye, a cherubic quality. Or is she more a gargoyle? If you came across her at rest, if it ever happens that she rests, she would appear quite pretty in a pouty, pigeony way. But she is always on the alert and that means defensive. She has two modes, either chin in the air or shoulders hunched. Perhaps that's why she shrugs so often, to relieve the tension of those extremes. A nearly perpetual scowl. A little plump for today's standards, a little fuller in the chest than in other areas (which gives her the pigeony look), all of which combines to create a certain comicality out of her belligerence. Even he finds it impossible not to smile at times. Even he.

Brother Bernard has developed a habit of referring to himself, in his rehearsing, in the third person. This is because he watches himself as well as others. He is fated always to be aware of his own thoughts and actions and their folly.

Michele glares at Brother Bernard. She can feel his benevolence radiating in her direction. She hasn't spoken since Father Gregory introduced her to the woman whose name is Linda. She spoke very little during the introduction, for that matter, which had forced Father Gregory to make conversation. He'd remarked that she had no pork chops on her plate. "I visited the pigs this morning and grew to like them," she told him. She had the pleasure of watching Linda toy with the chunk of meat she'd just severed from her chop.

Doggedly she eats her meal.

"Please would you pass the salt?" Linda asks.

Michele acts as though Linda has interrupted her thoughts. It doesn't work. Any thoughts she might have had are similarly interrupted with little murmurs about tomatoes that taste so different from the ones you get in Safeway, and how odd it is to be offered three different kinds of pickles, and having two desserts to choose from, and how Linda is bound to go home ten pounds heavier. Of the many things I dislike about you, Michele thinks, the thing I dislike most is your murmuring. It isn't true. The thing she dislikes most is Linda's slenderness.

Proximity works wonders. In two days Michele and Linda are friends. They exchange information about themselves in a way Michele has only overheard other people do, in a way she has sneered at before, has rolled her eyes at before. In the hallways and the lunch room at high school she overheard these conversations, how I want and he wants and I say and she says, how I always wanted and I never wanted and I thought I said and I should have said. Now it's her turn. She says it all too; it's easy to say anything to Linda.

"I want to be a nun."

They have already discussed the fact that neither of them has religion. Michele is thrilled to find an adult who agrees with her.

"You want to try it on."

They are lolling on the grass in the shade of a crab apple tree. The crab apples are tinged with pink and give off a faint apple scent. Michele considers Linda's suggestion.

"Try it on. That's right. That's exactly what I want to do. I want to look like a nun and have nun-like fantasies."

A black ant is scuttling up her leg, between and over the bristles. She hasn't shaved for a week.

"I want black oxfords with heavy heels, black pantyhose, a straight navy skirt and a navy sweater and I want my hair cut short like a man's. I want a big cross to hang from a chain around my neck."

Her ankle tickles. Another ant.

"I want to act as much like a nun and think as much like a nun as possible."

"Is that why you're here?"

Linda is brushing them off too.

"I'm here because my parents started to wonder what I was going to do all summer before university starts. I couldn't find a job. Hardly anyone can. Obviously my parents thought it was going to be a long summer with me mooning around the house making them sad because I have no friends."

"You'd look cool dressed like a nun."

"Sure." She must say this with some disdain, must keep the hope out of her voice.

"Try it."

"Yeah?"

"If it's what you want."

Frail old Father Abbot drifts up to them. Usually they only see him when he wanders from table to table after meals with his little bucket of soapy water and a J-cloth, wiping off crumbs and milk.

This time he has something concealed in his hand. He smiles at Linda and asks Michele a question.

"What kind of cookies do monks like?"

Michele shrugs.

"Hermits." He holds out his hand and leaves a cookie on each of their palms.

Brother Bernard, while hoeing between potato hills, is contemplating recording a series of conversations he hopes to have with Michele. Mentally recording. He wouldn't take notes or use a tape recorder. He'd record their conversation mentally then write it up for eventual publication under some title like "The Religious Life and the Imitative Impulse." She turned up this morning for breakfast wearing a nun-like get up and with all her hair cut off. Ironically, she looks cute. The sweater is tight. Her hair is spiky. Brother Bernard fears the reaction of some of the brothers. Isn't the cross almost blasphemous?

The storekeeper looks up when the door opens. He's been thinking about the pretty woman who's staying at the abbey, idly thinking about her while doing the books. She walks into town every other day at least. She's getting bored at the abbey; it isn't only cigarettes and scotch she needs in town. Not that he's planning to supply much else. Just talk. A few smiles into the eyes. That's what she needs and they both enjoy that. But it isn't her; it's a weird looking girl.

"What can I do for you?"

He hasn't seen this one before. Can't be a nun; they don't look like this.

"Nail polish?"

"You'll have to get that at the drug store."

The girl hesitates.

"Bet you don't know where that is."

"No."

"I'll walk you over."

He walked the pretty woman over to the hotel bar the week before. He gets razzed about this extra service he supplies to the women guests from the abbey. He says he's just being friendly and he sort of means it, but he doesn't mind getting a laugh either.

"You're the first customer all day, you know that?"

"No."

"No, guess you couldn't know that. Come on then."

He holds the door for her and slips his arm along the small of her back, propelling her along but only for a few moments.

She's in love, she's in love. With a mature man. It's her secret; she isn't going to tell Linda. She's made six trips to the store in four days. Linda is talking about her childhood over tuna melts. It's Friday lunch time.

"When I was a kid I wanted to grow up to be really fat. I wanted to be a fat lady. That's because I tried it once and made everyone laugh. I'd never realized until then how much fun it is to make people laugh."

Michele is thinking how she likes him to look at her.

"It was for a circus my cousins and I put on one summer."

Michele is thinking how his look says – I *like* you.

"I was only four or five and had no talents, no tap dancing or singing like the others. I couldn't do cartwheels."

Just for a second Michele sees a tiny Linda with yellow hair tumbling head over heels but the image is replaced by his face, his lazy eyes on her. She knows he likes to look at her.

"I wanted to be the fat lady in the circus."

He makes her glad.

"My cousins said I couldn't be her; I was too thin. But I wouldn't be anything else. So to keep me quiet they put me into my aunt's dress and stuffed it with pillows."

She can't let him know how glad she is when he looks at her.

"My cousins stood me in front of a mirror to show me how dumb I looked, but I didn't care. I wasn't going to give up."

Can she?

"So they billed me as "The Fat Lady with the Thin Face." They made a sign and when it was my turn to go in front of the adults, they carried the sign out first, then I walked on. I stood in front of the audience and grinned, because I'd got my own way. They loved it. They laughed till they cried."

Brother Bernard sidles up to the table to say hello and stands shyly waiting to be acknowledged.

"You should always go for it, don't you think, Brother Bernard?"

Linda is kind as well as pretty. She wouldn't leave someone standing there for very long, waiting to be acknowledged.

"If there's something you really want?"

"Only those who will hazard going too far can possibly know how far they can go," Brother Bernard says, echoing, as accurately as he can, one of those British poets – he is not sure which one, but one of those who would not say such a thing lightly. Then he blushes at the thought of having said such a thing at all.

Later he worries that he should have come up with an on the other hand. Should he have said something about temptation?

Unfortunately we don't always want what's best for us.

What a wonderful smile from Michele, though, as if he'd handed her a bouquet.

The storekeeper holds the door for Geraldine, his wife. They join two other couples in the corner behind the pool tables. Just about every Friday night they get together in the hotel bar. The hotel owner hauls himself off his chair and brings them their beer.

The girl from the abbey is sitting on the bench along the far wall. She's pretending to watch TV. You can tell she's pretending; her face is dazed. She's got a glass in front of her with Coke in it and something else, by the look of her. She's probably under age. One of the women whispers to Geraldine.

"Get a load of Sister Charity."

Geraldine's too nice to reply in kind. She grins. "God, I worked hard today," she says, stretching her muscles.

The kid looks over once or twice and the storekeeper pretends not to notice. It's kinder not to notice, he feels, especially when he's with his wife.

The storekeeper's wife and one of the other women are playing pool. Michele knows he is looking at her. She can tell. Inside she hums – her whole body hums. In her centre there is the sweetest ache. The humming, the vibration that started when he walked in the door, rocks the ache, swings it back and forth and keeps it alive. He's looking at her while his wife plays pool.

The bench she sits on faces the window that overlooks the train tracks and elevators. When she first arrived the sun had almost set but was still burning too brilliantly to allow her to look out the window for more than a second at a time. Now the window is black and she has the feeling only this room exists in all the world. He's looking again. He ignored her for a while so his wife wouldn't be alerted, but now he can't stop looking at her. He likes to look at her so much.

She turns and catches his eye. He gives her one of those slow smiles. She smiles into her drink. This is fine. To think she was wasting her time mooning over Brother Cory. And what a contrast to those kids in the truck. She never did have much in common with other kids; now she knows why.

It's warm still, the moon is out and she can see far over the fields, though not all the way down the road to the abbey. The town is quiet, the street deserted except for his truck angle-parked at the corner in front of the store. She gave him ten minutes to drop off his wife and come back for her. How she knows this is the way it works she isn't sure. He's sitting in the truck, watching her.

She walks over slowly. She has no idea what she's going to say or do when she gets there.

He says hello, so she says hello.

"Nice night," he says.

He turns and faces forward, looking out the windshield at nothing. She thinks: he's going to let me make my own decision, no interference from him. She walks around the truck to the passenger's side, opens the door and climbs in beside him. She shuts the door softly and joins him in looking out the windshield. His windows are down and a breeze blows through so soft and sweet she feels it's inside her.

His wife comes out of the store. She locks the door then walks up to the passenger's side of the truck and smiles at Michele.

The storekeeper says, "Geraldine, I've offered this young lady a lift back to the abbey."

Geraldine says hi. She climbs in beside Michele.

They drive to the abbey with the strange girl between them. Geraldine is kind to her. She asks how long she's been at the abbey, how long she's staying, whether she's been to visit their little cathedral with its famous German paintings. She should go at sunset, Geraldine tells her, she should walk in and leave the doors open because the doors face west and the paintings look very beautiful in that light.

They drop her off at the dormitory and turn around in the parking lot.

"You bastard," Geraldine says. It's the last thing she says to him for two days.

Brother Bernard cycles up and down the side roads with his skirts bunched at the knees and an old fishing hat jammed on his head to keep the rain out of his eyes. Around every corner, over every little rise, he expects he'll see Michele.

Michele is walking in the rain. It's a warm rain and in the woods not much of it reaches her. At breakfast, in front of everyone, she did just the kind of thing that makes people say there's something wrong with her. And it's Linda's last day. She wanders along the path in the woods. It doesn't matter where she goes; she always fucks things up.

Brother Bernard tries the little cathedral. A person might go there for solace. He checks inside the confessionals, rehearsing as he goes.

All true confessions are made at night, to another human if one has no God.

If he could talk to Michele some evening, she might unburden her soul. From her defensiveness it's easy to see she expects to be criticized, she expects to be asked for explanations. She was shocked when that wasn't the response she got this morning. Father Gregory, the guestmaster, who wasn't there at the time, was the only one who asked for an explanation, and he asked Brother Bernard. Michele had already gone by then. No, everyone was concerned for her, Linda most of all. No one saw her anger building or knew where it came from. As he explained to Father Gregory, Michele and Linda were sitting opposite one another as usual when Michele yelled something (it was not really incomprehensible but Brother Bernard saw no reason to repeat her language and lower her in Father's eyes) and dumped her breakfast on Linda's lap. The brothers came running. Father Abbot brought his J-cloth and started cleaning up. Everyone was solicitous of them both. Michele went out crying and now no one can find her.

A hummingbird hangs in the air like a miniature helicopter. She steps toward it. The hummingbird flies off but then it returns. It's as green as the leaves; it disappears into the leaves and a few seconds later reappears. All along the path it keeps ahead of her, flying in fits and starts. Like a kid, stopping at everything bright. She decides to pretend it's leading her somewhere.

Our destination is preordained by our nature, but only in the widest sense. If our nature is open to God, we will find him. Dear God....

Brother Bernard is praying for Michele, in the way he prayed as a child, as if writing a letter. It's the only resource left him. She's been gone all day, she's missed lunch and supper. Linda has put off her departure. She wanted to talk to Michele before she leaves, but now she's lugging her suitcases to her car. She's packing her trunk.

The hummingbird takes Michele to Mary's shrine in the woods. "Hail Mary, Queen of Peace," she reads inscribed above the plaster figure of Mary. The hummingbird dips its miniscule beak into the snapdragons that bloom in jam jars at her feet. They were its real destination.

"Mary, Mother of God," Michele says. "You look too young for the job." Those were the words of the one employer who interviewed her for a summer job.

"In the end my immaculate heart will triumph." Those are the words at Mary's feet.

"Lucky you," Michele says.

The rain has stopped. The clouds have cleared. The sun is sliding down and the trees are letting only streaks of light through to the path. Michele, in her damp clothes, feels chilly. It's time to go back and find some way to apologize.

The pond is a surprise. No one told her about it. It isn't on the abbey map. It's like a secret pond, in an unknown clearing, a pretty little pond, brushed with the gold of the low sun, with rushes at the edges.

It's warmer in the clearing. She stands for several minutes looking at the pond then she takes off her clothes, hangs them on a branch, and wades in. This isn't something she really wants to do and at first it's disgusting. The soft mud sucks at her toes and her feet sink almost to the ankles. But she is doing this as she would climb up on another horse. That's how she thinks of it. She believes what Linda and Brother Bernard told her; she'll never know how far she can go if she won't take risks. Her entire body shudders as her foot sinks once again on its way to the bottom.

Linda has gone to the guest lounge for a coffee before she departs. Brother Bernard says he'll have a last look in the woods behind the gymnasium. Linda says she thinks Michele doesn't want to be found, but Brother Bernard thinks she will want to atone, or at least that she'll be sorry later if she misses the chance.

She is up to her neck and the water settles around her in layers, warmest at her neck, cool down to her legs, cold at her knees, and warm again at her feet. She turns this way and that. The water tugs at the hair between her legs. The water is golden-streaked and strange long-legged insects skate across it. She turns and turns.

Brother Bernard hurries past the statue of Mary.

Wading out of the pond, she feels the water falling off her.

Halfway between the statue and the pond, he halts. Though his inclination is to forge ahead, Brother Bernard goes back to pay his respects to Mary, to say a short prayer for Michele and another for himself, for the doubt that has slipped in and mingled with his good intentions. A hummingbird is drinking from a snapdragon close to his knee. He sees how fast its wings have to beat to keep its body in the air and he thinks that's how fast a person has to pray to keep believing.

She is cool again and dresses quickly. She should find Linda and apologize.

Hurrying past the pond to the path that leads out of the woods, Brother Bernard comes on Michele. She is sitting on her haunches.

"Look what I've found," she says.

Wild strawberries.

She hands him a few and stands. She thinks, finally I've got a man in the berries and look who it is.

Brother Bernard thinks she's almost beautiful but he's much too shy to tell her so. She is giving him a very peculiar look. For a second he thinks it's lascivious but it's not that. It's the absence of something that is peculiar. The darts are gone from her eyes. He's been calling them darts because he's seen that she has a liveliness (you might even call it mischief at times) inside her that she tries to hide behind averted eyes or belligerent stares, and this liveliness darts out at others quite often in spite of her desire to hide it.

A person, finding himself the recipient of these darts, may feel they are in response to him, to a humanity, a kinship she recognizes in him, perhaps. He may feel that he has stimulated her in some way so that she must let the darts fly and fall as they may.

Brother Bernard supposes he calls them darts, too, because they sometimes mysteriously hurt.

There are no darts in this look. It is simply Michele, looking at him. No mischief. No defences. No expectations. He is looking into her face, into her eyes, and she is letting him see *her*.

Here is what excites him most: there are no words.

Of course by the time he's thinking all this, it's over and she is asking whether Linda has left yet and he's telling her if they move quickly they may catch her before she goes.

Follow me, he says, and tears off.

Hiking up his skirts to facilitate his progress over the odd fallen twig on the path out of the woods...

Michele is behind him. His thoughts race ahead.

He has made a great discovery. He has witnessed a soul bared, and there were no words. No words needed.

He's heard of this before, of course.

Words must be eschewed; the communication can only be non-verbal.

But he hasn't experienced it before. Surely it can't be a common experience. He must write something on it. He might work it into his paper on "The Religious Life and the Imitative Impulse." It won't be a series of conversations, as he'd first planned. He and Michele haven't had any – a series of non-conversations, he might call it. A highly experimental piece, perhaps breaking new ground.

Linda's trunk is packed. Father Gregory walks her back to her car, which sits in the lot facing the road home. This was her first visit to the abbey and it will be her last. She hasn't found any peace. She has only been bored and restless and a spoiler. Father Gregory is telling her about the newspaper they publish at the abbey and she is murmuring responses. She's good at small talk and doesn't need to think to keep it up.

She can think her own thoughts, which are troubled. She thought she was just what the girl needed, a sympathetic adult, someone to encourage her to open up, to face the world without defences. She should not have given advice to a kid who is obviously confused. Whatever upset Michele, if it had something to do with those stupid conversations about going all out for what you want, she's responsible. It's bad advice,

Linda thinks, remembering her own humiliation. She blushes to think of it. She pretty much offered herself to the village storekeeper and got turned down. Standing by her car door, listening to Father Gregory talk about the problems of editing some of the more enthusiastic submissions he receives, she blushes all over her face and down her neck.

Brother Bernard dashes out of the woods with Michele behind him. They startle several of Father Abernathy's graphologists who are walking into town for a beer. Brother Bernard spares an instant's pity for them.

If words are nearly useless in matters of the spirit, how hollowly trivial is the handwriting in which the words are recorded?

He might work up a paper on that subject as well, when Father Abernathy has returned to California.

Father Gregory, still talking to the charming pretty woman, has noticed Brother Bernard hastening out of the woods toward them. He has seen Michele running behind him. Her cross bouncing on her chest. Father Gregory grins. She looks as cute as a button, he thinks. It's a phrase his mother used to use. He wonders where it comes from. Michele is waving and calling to Linda. He's very pleased to see it.

When Brother Bernard and Michele reach them, Father Gregory says goodbye to give Michele and Linda a chance to talk.

"Brother Bernard," he says, "just the man I was looking for." He leads Brother Bernard off toward the buildings. "Good work, Brother Bernard," he says, once they're out of earshot.

He is listening to Father Gregory but thoughts come to him.

Is the idea of the love of God a fantasy of the religious? Could the same idea be phrased by the secular as a feeling of belonging in nature? Had he come upon Michele in a secular prayer?

Intuitively he rejects the equivalence. Even with his mind half on what Father is saying, when he thinks of God's love he thinks of an area around his head, and when he thinks of belonging to nature, he envisions his feet. Not at all the same thing. Although of course this sort of concrete thinking would be unacceptable in academic circles, it will form the basis of every argument he makes in this regard for the rest of his life. He knows this. Furthermore, he believes it's the same for everyone, even if only the naïve would admit it. He is very happy suddenly.

He is as a child, and for some things, that is good.

Linda's face is red. Michele thinks she must be very angry with her. Usually when people get angry with her, Michele gets angry back, but not this time. It makes her feel really nervous and almost strangles her, but she says she's sorry.

Behind the parking lot is a cornfield and behind that a dozen or so pine trees make a row of dark spikes. They remind Linda of the monks. If the monks put their cowls up when they filed to mass or whatever ritual it is that takes them three or four times a day to chant in the chapel, they would look like that. Around the pine trees and around the monks she sees wavy lines of motion. A Van Gogh painting. Swirling. She can't bear to be here another second. She can't wait to get into her car and drive away from here. It's pity, pity swirling around her, for people who will never, never learn.

As soon as she's on the road, she jabs at the radio buttons until she finds music no one in this part of the world would listen to, music that belongs in a smoky basement dive, to people who think they've seen it all. She turns the volume up, buzzes down her windows, passes every vehicle in her path.

Song of Songs

In Paris they were told: "It is not possible." In rural France: "It will be difficult." That was if they could find anyone to speak English to them. In Italy they were laughed at. But they got where they wanted to go, or where she wanted to go, most of the time. They were travelling by train on what he called the vacation of a lifetime, meaning he wasn't going to do it again.

On a Sunday in October they were sitting on the second of three trains that were supposed to take them from a little fishing village called Vernazza, just south of the Italian Riviera, to a border town called Ventimiglia, and from there to Nice. Jack said he thought they were on the wrong train. That made Reni mad. If they were on the wrong train it was his fault. He'd acted as if he knew what he was doing. If they weren't on the wrong train, he was being an alarmist, pessimistically predicting disaster at every turn instead of looking on their trip as an adventure, instead of being fun. If it had been up to him, he'd have turned back at every ticket window where he'd heard the word "difficult," to say nothing of "impossible," and they wouldn't have been half the places they'd been or seen half the things they'd seen.

Jack said if they were on the wrong train, they wouldn't be stopping at Nice once they found the right train. He said by the time they got to Nice, it would be too late to make it to the Chagall museum, which was Reni's only reason for going to Nice in the first place.

"It's open in the morning," she said.

"If there's an afternoon train to Paris," he said.

"We're not in the boondocks here," she said.

"It'll be a rush," he said.

She thought she heard satisfaction in his voice.

"Don't forget we have to be at the airport first thing the next morning," he said. "Don't forget Air France is on strike."

"We're going Air Canada."

He opened his spy novel. He wasn't going to explain all the complications that were bound to occur because of the strike. She'd call him a pessimist, she'd act as if he'd planned the strike to show her how much trouble he had to go through to get her from A to B. People had been shot at during this strike; the strikers were carrying guns. Planes were rerouted, flights cancelled, but she expected to sail through it all.

They were not on the wrong train. This Jack discovered by asking a conductor, who sneered at him for being worried about such a puny eventuality as being on the wrong train, headed in the wrong direction.

Jack closed his eyes and fell asleep. His head swayed toward the nun who was sitting beside him. Her eyes were closed too, but Reni didn't believe she was sleeping. She believed the nun had closed her eyes to hide from them.

Jack's head tilted, then jerked upright. "Uh," he said, and settled back into the seat. Reni remembered a girl who'd shared a compartment with them on one of their trips, who'd gone through a cleansing ritual before she'd sat down, scrubbing the seat with one of those alcohol-and-detergent-soaked paper cloths out of a foil packet. Reni wondered if Jack was getting head lice now. She wondered if she was. On another trip they'd sat across the aisle from a young couple who had made her want to scream. The young man had insisted on pulling the young woman's head into his lap. When she struggled and protested, he pushed it down and gripped it between his knees. He then picked lice out of her hair. Reni knew that was what he was doing because she'd seen monkeys doing it on television. He was more like a monkey than a human, she thought, small and swarthy, gypsy-looking with a bandana tied around his head. She hated him for the way he treated the young woman, but also for the way he treated *her* and the other passengers, subjecting them all to his animal version of humanity. She saw that the other passengers were looking down their noses at him and at the girl too, and she hated him for making her hate him, and for making her suspect that she was only a hair's breadth to the left of being a racist in her opinion of him. She wanted to blink and find him gone. She wanted it enough she was afraid to blink. But this is what travel does for you, she told herself, calming her remembered anger; to travel is to learn, as much about yourself as anything. How smug she was, efficiently consigning her disturbing memory to the educational.

She turned her attention to the nun beside Jack, who seemed to be sleeping for real now, serene in her grey and black bird's uniform, her wings folded and clipped. Reni had always thought nuns mysterious creatures. Examining this woman, she came to no conclusions; the mystery was neither expanded nor dispelled but remained present in the nun, in her clipped-ness. Reni tried to define for herself what she meant by that term. She closed her eyes to think better and pulled her arms closer to her sides, her knees closer together – thinking with her body, but not for long. The train vibrated, it swung along the tracks as if it would at any moment swing off. Her arms slowly opened, her hands sank into the dirty upholstery, her knees parted.

The cessation of motion woke all three travellers an hour later. They had come to Ventimiglia.

It was raining in Nice. The entire south of France was flooded. Tourists were going elsewhere, except for those who hadn't heard the news for weeks. In the entire hotel owned and operated by Jean-Luc and Sylvie Duverger – a two star hotel of modest pretensions, of twenty-two rooms – only one room was occupied. One couple was paying money to stay with them, and that couple Jean-Luc hated. His wife Sylvie didn't hate them, but then it was possible she hated no one, unless Jean-Luc had taught her finally to hate him. She was a slow learner; quick at her actions – she was chopping onions now like a television chef – but slow to learn. The opposite of him, in fact. He was vacuuming the dining room, but anyone watching him would think he was pushing the thing around as an aid to his ruminations. He was a most philosophical cleaner; when he deigned to vacuum at all he vacuumed as he was certain Jean Paul Sartre, whom he had met once, would have vacuumed if he had had to run a failing hotel in Nice.

The couple Jean-Luc hated were from England. The man was a nonentity. The woman had a red face, she was fat and spoke French with the usual enthusiasm of tourists who speak it badly. It was not Jean-Luc's role in life to improve the French of tourists; he answered invariably in English. But this one kept babbling on. Her husband had just enough sense to be occasionally embarrassed for her, though since he had too little personality to shut her up, his apportionment of sense counted for nothing.

Sylvie was replenishing the soup pot. At the same time she was keeping an eye on the syrup for the *crème caramel*. He was a devil if she burnt it and had to throw it out. He was vacuuming the dining room to be in the vicinity if she burnt it this time; he suspected she wasted food with every meal she made. It wasn't easy to keep up the pretense of "*cuisine traditionelle et soignée*" on the budget he gave her. It wasn't her idea to spend their money putting television sets with *Canal* and direct telephones in every room. The bathrooms she could see. Americans demanded them. The televisions and telephones had done them no good. All her hard work and his disdain of their guests had done them no good. She set her mouth and bent her head to her onions. Unconsciously, she shrugged.

A bang from the dining room brought her running from her chopping. A table was overturned; the vacuum cleaner was overturned; Jean-Luc was galloping through the room, his cigarette clenched in his teeth. The dog skittered ahead of him. He'd tripped on poor Claude, that was the cause of this farce. "Claude, Claude!" she called, but too late. Jean-Luc had him in the corner. He took aim while the animal cringed; he kicked him and she said nothing, standing in a strip of pale sunlight between the kitchen and the dining room, with a knife in her hand.

It was raining in Nice and they didn't have a hotel. It was Reni's idea that they didn't need reservations on this trip, that reservations would only tie them down. Jack planned never to travel again without reservations, if he were ever so weak as to travel again. He had a feeling

Nice was going to prove his point. The tourist information office was closed, so was the hotel reservation office.

"Open bright and early tomorrow morning," he pointed out.

She had the names and addresses of two hotels in their price range, not too far from the railway station. She didn't have a map. They slung their matching duffel bags over their shoulders and set out.

"It's only drizzling," she said.

He pointed to a hotel across the street. She said the area near the station was reputed to be unsafe at night. He said it looked to be well on its way by day. There was a Sunday emptiness to the streets; few people were on the sidewalks and those they encountered they would rather have evaded. Mostly they were large males of the species, seemingly on the loose and aggressively alien. Reni had to remind herself she and Jack were the foreigners here. As for Jack, like any red-blooded Canadian male out of his depth, he avoided eye contact.

They rejected the first hotel they checked out, a one star three blocks from the station. Reni didn't like the pencil-width gap between the door and its frame. She didn't get as far as the toilet, which was just as well, Jack thought. She wouldn't have liked it either.

"They never even vacuum these places," she whispered as they slipped down the stairs, and Jack steeled himself to say no to the hotel owner and receive the obligatory sneer to his manhood.

After that Reni started looking for a two star. They trudged into a marginally better area and the hotels leapt from one to three. They made a U-turn. Their bags (pack light and you won't be sorry) were getting heavier and they didn't know where they were or where they were going. Just then, the rain increased and the wind got up. It was like walking through a low-budget movie set in a seedy neighbourhood, Jack thought. *Film Noir*. Awnings flapped over their heads, wet pieces of paper cruised the wind and pasted themselves against the shop windows. Just for a second, Ingrid Bergman was possible.

Jack looked at his watch. It was nearly two. "What time does the Chagall museum close?" he asked.

"Fuck off," Reni said.

He tugged her under an awning and took her bag from her. She leaned into the wall, tired out. They'd been on the move since five-thirty in the morning. "We could take the bags back to the station," he said. "Take a cab to the museum, and find a hotel afterwards. We're only here to see those Chagalls, right?"

"Right," she said. She was not so sure the Chagalls mattered any more.

"Right," he said. "Now where are we?"

He looked up for a street sign, thinking at the same time that knowing the name of the street wasn't going to be much help in finding the station.

"Reni," he said. "Look up."

She leaned out from under the awning and looked up, as he was doing, into the rain. Above the awning was a hotel sign, with two stars.

There was something about travelling that made Reni feel irrational at times, and this was one of those times. A picture of her childhood God loomed above her, his long and bony finger pointing at the hotel door. She supposed she was experiencing a state of extreme gratitude.

They had to ring a buzzer to get into the hotel. The door was opened by a slight, very French-looking man with one enlarged car.

"Bonjour," they said, in unison.

"Hello. Come in," he said. He moved back with the door and ushered them with his free hand in the only possible direction they could take, along a narrow hallway toward the reception desk. He answered yes to all Jack's questions. It was an amused kind of yes; he might have been saying, "but yes," "but yes"; they might have been placed on earth at this moment for his entertainment. Once behind the desk, he smiled toward his wife; it seemed he meant to share his enjoyment of Jack and Reni with her. She was sitting at a small round table in an alcove off the reception area, an alcove so French to Reni's mind – dim and doilied and shabby – that she breathed deeply in appreciation. The couple had obviously been having their lunch; there was red wine in their glasses, bread in a dish between the two plates, his chair pushed back, a dog on the floor at her feet. The woman looked up from her plate as if her husband had called her. Attuned to him, Reni thought and then, although she understood that the amusement was supposed to be one-sided (or maybe because she understood), she got the giggles. The word "attuned" rang in her mind;

she couldn't help thinking about the man's ear (what could he tune in with that thing?) and had to cover with a pretended fit of coughing. The hotel owner raised his eyebrows and suggested they follow him.

"It's quite clean," Reni said. They were sprawled on the bed for a five-minute rest before tackling the trek to the museum. She did not refer to her attack of the giggles; she didn't think Jack would appreciate it, and it didn't show her in too good a light, after all. "Did you notice how French they are?" she asked.

Jack had noticed that the room was going to set them back about eighty dollars Canadian and that the guy had a big ear with a cotton ball in it, not much else.

"It's just like a Georges Simenon novel," Reni said. "*Just* like one."

Jack had not read a Georges Simenon novel, but he knew whatever "it" was, it was what Reni had been looking for and not found in the two weeks they'd already spent in France. He sighed and closed his eyes. He often said his only aim in life was to make her happy. It wasn't easy. She was too optimistic in her expectations, she wanted too much, grabbed at experiences. He'd watched her in Venice; he'd seen her face when she came walking up out of that subway in Milan to the sight of the Duomo flying off the pavement. She was flying too. The problem was, she could crash. Something could go wrong and put her lower than you'd believe possible. He had to work to keep her on the up side.

"Better get a move on," he said.

Sylvie came out of the kitchen with her table brush and pan just as the Americans came down the stairs. She bent her head and stopped to let them pass. She knew Jean-Luc was watching her from behind the desk, pretending to read his newspaper. She gave the couple a shy smile. They went to the desk to ask the way to the Chagall Museum. That made Jean-Luc happy. He liked giving directions and especially he liked showing that he was cultured. Probably he would tell them he'd met Chagall once. Maybe he had. She wouldn't know, would she? She brushed the crumbs off the tablecloth into her pan. The dog thumped its tail but didn't get up. Poor old Claude. Poor Claude, poor Claude. And that ear of Jean-Luc's, it was suppurating again. What a mess. What a fool she was to have married the man. You'd think the ear itself would have turned her off – if not his alienation from every living thing – but she had thought she was being noble, she had thought she was marrying for love. An ear like that, ugly though it was, meant nothing to her. She was marrying the man for himself, not for two perfect ears. But if she had known that it often got infected because it was deformed inside and out – as he was – that pus came out of it, that it would disgust her to think of it, that he would kick her poor old dog....

Now he was joking with the Americans. Haw! Haw! After they left he would call them donkeys. She hurried back into the kitchen to separate eggs so that by the time he came in, she'd have the mixer going to make her meringues, and could pretend she didn't hear him.

Reni was disappointed in *The Biblical Message*. She was tired when they got there. They'd waited twenty minutes for a bus that hadn't come and then walked the distance to the museum, which took them over half an hour. The rain had stopped, but it had left the city looking dirty and dull. The museum was crowded with a lot of pushy people speaking French. Reni stood in line for a good fifteen minutes to get a *petit guide* in English, while Jack leaned against a wall. When she discovered, on walking into the first room, that the paintings were not hung in the order outlined in the guide book that had just cost her ten dollars (on top of twenty-eight dollars admission for the two of them), she started looking for a human sacrifice. Jack saw that look in her eyes, and feared it would have to be him.

No, she didn't like *The Biblical Message*, although Chagall, according to the guide book, considered this group of paintings the highest expression of his "dream." There was something mechanically spiritual about them, if such a thing was possible. Huge and bright as they were, and though she sat on a bench in the first room, trying to ignore the annoyance of their being either hung in the wrong order or described in the wrong order, trying to be awed by them, she was not awed. His colours were there: his blue, his red, his sulfurous yellow, and his symbols – cocks all over the place, flying horses and trees – but the people all looked limp. They looked barely able to cope in all the chaos. They looked sad in the presence of angels, and all too ready to kill their only son who looked all too ready to die. Jacob appeared to be giving his angel a blow job rather than wrestling with him, and in every painting of Moses he looked more like a snail than a leader of men. Where were the lovers? It was the lovers she loved and they were missing here. Only in one painting, almost hidden in the dark bottom corner of what she thought might be "The Creation of Man," was there a tiny couple, but the most they could summon in the way of emotion was a futile sort of tenderness. She could have cried in this room, sitting on a vinyl bench with French words and French people milling around her. Where were the lovers, the brides and grooms, the married couples? The women, a little aloof, proud of their power. The men, head-over-heels, goofy with love. It was a refreshing vision. Untheoretical love.

Jack pried her off the bench and led her from room to room. He pointed out the architecture; the museum was designed and built for the collection. He pointed out the mosaic, Elijah reflected in the pool beneath him. They sat for a few minutes in the concert hall where she couldn't help responding to the blue light of the three stained glass windows. A pair of children played tag up and down the aisles, giggling and yelping, so it was not, in spite of the intensity of the light, an inspirational experience. They moved on to the Song of Songs paintings, hung in a hexagonal room. She liked these ones better; the people in them were not quite so "palely loitering," and there were lovers, but they were still frail, elongated, drawn out by circumstances, drifting and decorous. All the reds combined couldn't give them life. From what she remembered of Solomon's version of the songs, Reni told Jack, she would have expected less of heaven and more of earth. She and her friends, in the time they were taking confirmation classes, which would have been about grade six, had laboured over the Song of Songs, squeezing it for sexual allusions, making fun of the comparisons (thy teeth are like a flock of sheep) and swooning over its beauty. The one verse they all memorized, the only one she could remember now, was the famous "Thou hast ravished my heart, my sister, my spouse! how much better is thy love than wine!" She had repeated it so many times to her pubescent self, imagining a lover looking into her eyes and saying it, that she couldn't have said it aloud, now, without blushing.

On their way back to the hotel, they looked for a restaurant and didn't find one that suited them. They decided to try dinner at their hotel. They were both ready for an early night.

The dog was underfoot as usual. Jean-Luc swore and the cur whimpered and shuffled off to his rug in the lounge. Jean-Luc had tables to set and he set every table though often only one was needed, for the couple who ate breakfast and dinner with them every day. He left a curl of ash on the table where he intended seating the English couple, if they stayed in for dinner. The dog wandered into the room again. The thing was stupid. Its hair hung in its eyes. Its nails clicked on the board floor. Jean-Luc put down his stack of napkins and took the creature by the scruff of the neck. He hauled him through the kitchen to the back door. The leash was hanging on its nail. He clipped it to the collar. The dog perked up as soon as they were outside, looked up and down the alley and sniffed his way to the garbage cans. Jean-Luc walked on and the leash pulled Claude along. Jean-Luc knocked at a back door at the intersection of the alley and the street. A boy answered.

"Ten francs for you if you keep this mutt till midnight," Jean-Luc told the boy.

"Okay."

Rain started to fall again before Jean-Luc reached the hotel. Sylvie was in the kitchen when he came in. "You're wet," she said. He didn't answer.

"And how did you find the Chagall museum?" the hotel owner asked.

"It was right where you said it would be," Jack said.

The man got a pained expression on his face.

"Very beautiful," Reni said.

"Yes," he said. (But yes. Of course: it is French.) "Brotherhood and love, yes? The message of Marc Chagall to all men."

"I suppose he meant Siblinghood," Reni said.

"Pardon?"

"Reni's little joke," Jack said.

They arranged to have dinner at seven, which was when the dining room opened, and went up to their room to wait out their hunger for an hour.

"Siblinghood," Jack said, when they were not quite out of hearing of the front desk. He laughed all the way to the room.

Sylvie ladled soup into bowls for the English couple. Jean-Luc came up from the cellar with a bottle of cheap wine for the Americans.

"Jean-Luc?"

But he ignored her. He set the wine down and marched off with the soup as if he cared whether the English received it hot. When he returned to the kitchen, she tried again. "Jean-Luc, where is Claude?" He was wiping the wine bottle. He didn't pretend not to hear her; he just didn't answer. He wiped out two wineglasses. That was to tell her he was fastidious, she was not.

"I'm ravenous," Reni said.

"The soup smells good."

The hotel owner appeared with their wine and proceeded to open the bottle.

"Could we get some bread?" Jack asked.

"Yes. Would Monsieur taste the wine?"

Jack did as he was told. He had drunk more wine on this trip than in all his life; still, he could barely tell the difference between white and red. But he nodded and grinned at Reni.

It was necessary for them to order their meals, apparently, before they could get bread.

"The soup's very nice," a British voice called from across the room. The large red-faced woman was beaming at them. Her husband, a surprisingly handsome elderly gentleman, nodded his agreement, for his mouth was full.

"I'll have the soup," Jack said. "And the special."

"*Plat du jour*," the owner murmured.

"Right."

Reni couldn't make up her mind about a first course. The owner recommended the tomato and mozzarella salad.

"I've had lots of that," Reni said. "We've just spent two weeks in Italy."

"How unfortunate for you," he murmured.

"Oh, we loved Italy!" she said.

"Where did you visit in Italy?" the British woman hollered. Reni started listing all the places they'd visited.

"You'd better bring the bread," Jack said to the owner.

"As you wish," the man said. He picked up Jack's menu and walked off. Half an hour passed before he approached their table again. During that time he fussed over the third and last couple to eat in the dining room that evening. This couple was given a prime window location. They intrigued Reni, who had been seated looking out into the room and watched them when she wasn't talking to the English couple. She changed her mind several times in the course of the evening about whether the two being fussed-over were a man and a woman or two men or two women. They were the most completely androgynous people she'd ever seen. She thought she learned a lot about her own attitudes by testing what she considered clues to their sex. She was able to devote only a small portion of her attention to them, however, because their own conversation with the English couple budded as they drank their wine on empty stomachs and then bloomed full out when they all four got going on their second bottles.

The English couple came from the area where *Lovejoy* was filmed. *Lovejoy* being one of both men's favourite television shows, they established a bond of mutual admiration. The woman told them she'd been coming to this particular hotel in Nice since she was very young. She used to stay here alone, she said, on a little holiday alone, every year. She was about sixty-five, Reni guessed, and she said the hotel had changed a good deal. Reni said she thought it very French, very quaint. "Oh, my dear," the woman said. "If you think it's French now!" They talked on about the hotel, what it was like all those years ago, and Reni speculated in a parallel inner conversation on what the woman had been doing here, and whether she had really been alone. Was it possible she was reliving an annual affair, almost celebrating it, in front of her husband? Reni had never done such a thing as go on a holiday alone. She was thrilled by all the mysteries, not only of this woman having done it, but of her daily life while doing it. (How did she fill the hours if she really was alone?) These mysteries, and the deeper mysteries of the other couple by the window, led her to think how mysterious even Jack was to her, even, to some extent, how mysterious she was to herself, which lead to the conclusive thought: how wonderful it was to be alive and a little drunk on a night like this.

Jack, having seen the faraway look, pressed her knee with his. He had planned to save himself (and her) for a last romantic night in Paris. At their age, you couldn't count on two nights in a row being entirely successful. But he could see the big night was going to be tonight. He refilled her wine glass.

They all got steadily louder. After weeks of keeping their apologetic English at a low level, and with a feeling of burning their bridges, because they were heading home in less than forty hours, Reni and Jack bandied banalities, finding themselves as well as the others increasingly hilarious. They wolfed down their food, when it finally came, smacking their lips and groaning their approval. They began to find the hotel owner hilarious, too. That started when Reni, in innocence, said, "Chagall wasn't French, was he?" and the owner answered, "Only by inclination, Madame." For some reason all four of them hooted and then laughed so hard the tears ran down their faces. After that, they were out of control. The poor man couldn't walk past them disdainfully without sending them into fits. When their wine was gone, it was all they could do to haul themselves off their chairs and hie off to bed, the four of them red-faced, the women with mascara on their cheeks, the men clapping each other on the back on the way up the stairs.

Reni was walking about the room, throwing off clothes. "Those lovers were all wrong," she said.

Jack was cutting a toenail and didn't answer.

"Tell me about it," she imagined him saying, and then she was kneeling at his feet – no, he knelt at her feet – they knelt, facing one another.

He said, "Thou hast ravished my heart."

She said, "Your love is better than wine."

No. She flung off her brassiere and strutted around the bed. "My tits are like towers!" she exclaimed.

He put the nail clippers down, jumped to his feet and strutted with her. Imitating the roosters in the Chagall paintings. "Just think of me as a cock," he said.

No. But he went to the bathroom and washed and brushed his teeth and when he came back he was a little subdued, as if he too would have liked to have been outrageous. By that time, she had poured them each a little glass of Calvados (as if they needed it) and when he slid into bed beside her and picked his glass up, she raised hers and said, "Here's looking at you, kid." He didn't protest that he'd already brushed his teeth. He laughed at her and drank his brandy.

Sylvie let herself into the hotel. She had exhausted herself walking through the wet, glittering streets. She had not been bothered. She had known, setting out, that she was safe, that her grief would protect her.

When she was cooking the steaks, Jean-Luc had finally told her that Claude was dead.

"Where is he?" she asked.

"Where do you think?"

He left the kitchen. She watched the steaks, of course. You could not overcook steaks. She cried a little for her old dog. She finished her cooking and did her cleaning up. He went to the lounge to sit and smoke and fume about the English and Americans, about their nonchalance and happiness, about their larger slice of pie. She scrubbed her counters and put away her pots and pans. She got sadder as they got louder, but she didn't begrudge them their fun; the lack in her life couldn't be attributed to them. "Now Claude is gone," she said to herself over and over – just that, as she cleaned and put away.

"I'm going to bed," she told him when he returned to the kitchen, and she meant to go to bed. She went to their suite. She was sad, it was true. She was thinking: Claude is gone. She was not thinking what Jean-Luc wanted her to think, that Jean-Luc had killed him, but now she was alone with no work to do, of course she began to think of that. Then her sadness for the loss of the dog became a sadness for everything that was gone.

She went out walking because it was required of her: some sign of capitulation. He would usher the guests out of the dining room and turn his feet toward their suite. He would find the suite empty and be thrilled that he had sent her out. It would be a satisfaction to him, after the evening he'd endured. He would know as well as she that she'd come back.

When she was walking, it came to her that she was looking for something. She must be looking for something because she didn't pass through the streets in a daze; she looked ahead, she wondered about what she'd see around corners. She was surprised at herself; she didn't know what she had to look for. Some sign perhaps, but she didn't find it.

When she let herself into the hotel, she stood in the dark hallway, listening, but she heard nothing. It was close enough to morning she decided to go to the kitchen and begin her baking. She looked into the lounge on her way to the kitchen, looked to the rug where Claude had slept for nearly ten years, and he was there. He raised his head and looked at her. Absurdly, she thought: you're not much of a guard dog, old Claude. She went into the lounge and sat on the floor beside him. He lay his head in her lap and gave her his brown-eyed gaze. For some time she sat without thinking, stroking the dog, aware only of his warmth and his eyes on hers. Then her hand discovered the skin and bones under his fur, felt the skin move under hers, over his bones. Of course, she had been looking for Jean-Luc; she had thought (no, not thought, not even hoped), she had wished he would come out looking for her; he would say nothing of course, but they would have one of their reconciliations. She had realized that the laughter of the English and American couples was taunting to him and that she would be expected to suffer for it. She had thought she was the stronger, but he was going to win against her, she could see that now. He had almost unbalanced her, with this. The next time, or the time after that, she would not think of him, of his suffering, only of herself. She buried her head into Claude's neck. She lay down on the rug beside him and drew him to her.

Reni and Jack were skipping breakfast so they could catch the early TGV that would get them into Paris before two. Otherwise, Jack pointed out, they'd get into the city at about five, which meant rush hour in the Metro and they'd have their bags to carry. They'd settled with the owner the night before. Jack had been efficient enough to think of that. Coming downstairs, they were hoping they could slip out unnoticed. They were slightly embarrassed about their behaviour the night before. However, the hotel owner and his wife were having breakfast at their small table in the lounge (*croissants* and *café au lait*, what else, and they smelled out of this world), so it was necessary to stop and say good-bye. Both the man and his wife rose from their chairs. The dog stood too and came and sniffed around them.

"You are off then?" the hotel owner asked.

"To Paris," Jack said. "Have you heard any more about the strike?"

"They are still on strike," the man said. "We are plagued by strikes in this country."

"It's a beautiful country," Reni said. "We've loved being here."

"Nice hotel you have here," Jack said. "Great *crème caramel*, by the way," he said to the wife. "Best we had the whole trip, and I can tell you, we're connoisseurs by now."

"Thank you," she said.

"Really great," Jack said.

"I am happy you like it," she said.

Just as it was beginning to seem to Reni that they would never get out of the hotel, that they were in some kind of social purgatory, and their punishment was to stay in this lobby forever repeating niceties, the hotel owner took it upon himself to usher them out the door. Even then, they turned and waved, and the owner and his wife nodded, with more dignity, Reni was relieved to see, than she and Jack could muster.

In Paris that evening they went to the Museum of Modern Art at Beaubourg centre, to get out of the cold and rain and to see the view as much as the art. The view was spectacular. The light rain didn't hide the city; it made it shine. They rode the escalators to the top and stood leaning against the railings, looking at the glittering Eiffel Tower with the shining streets shooting out from it.

They liked this gallery. They worked their way thoughtfully through the rooms. Reni mentioned only once how few women were exhibited.

They were beginning to tire, and to think of the long trek back to their hotel, when they rounded a corner and nearly walked into a large vertical Chagall.

"There they are," Reni said. The lovers. A bride and a groom, as large as life and twice as happy, as her mother would have said. The groom was sitting on the bride's shoulders, waving aloft a glass of red wine. The bride stood with her feet braced, her breasts spilling out of her gown. The couple were almost toppling, but they wouldn't topple.

"There they are," Reni said again. She laughed. "We didn't need to stop in Nice," she said.

"Right," Jack said. He was thinking about tomorrow. His mind was on the strike, on how he was going to get them out of the country as painlessly as possible.

She saw that preoccupied look on his face and took his arm. "We'd better go," she said. "We need to make an early start tomorrow."

He was pleased and let her see it. She was pleased to have pleased him. He put his arm around her and they zoomed downward on the escalator, past the dark and shimmering city. At the street level, he held the glass door open for her.

"Which way?" she asked, turning her face up to him. He kissed her – in a public, well-lit square with people around. Something he would not have done at home. She raised her eyebrows in mock surprise.

Carlyle's House

For three weeks one year in June, Muriel was hired as a temporary caretaker in Carlyle's house. She was hired to relieve the curator and his wife while they went on holidays. She had no qualifications for the job and got it only because she was the curator's second cousin and was thought by him to be reliable. During her time at Carlyle's house, she lapsed once into irresponsibility. She played a trick on a visitor, a small, mean trick. Muriel thinks she knows why she did it: out of an older woman's disdain for her younger self's ambition. But there are things that aren't clear.

Some things aren't clear to Elizabeth either. Quite a few, in fact. She isn't sure she wants clarification. She visited Carlyle's house one day, one year in June, and a woman played a trick on her. This was a long time ago; she doesn't think of it often but when she does, she wonders if she could have done something different and what the outcome would have been.

In preparation for living in the house and assisting tourists, Muriel had read some of Carlyle's work (*Sartor Resartus*, at least) and a couple of biographies. The biographies naturally made her curious about Jane Carlyle. At the time she moved into the house to take over, to the limited extent possible for her, the duties of the curator and his wife, she began to read the two collections of Jane's letters. Like others before her, she read with fascination. Bits of information and innuendo tantalized her; she was drawn to read on. The next letter or the one after that might reveal the whole woman, the complete picture of an educated, talented, witty author who revealed her pettiness a thousand times, yet left her reader wishing to know her.

Of all the relationships discussed and implied in the letters, those between the Carlyles and their servants intrigued Muriel most. Especially, she found herself interested in Jane's attitude toward one servant, a girl of fifteen called Charlotte who had come to live in the house when Jane was in her fifties. Muriel herself was in her fifties that summer she lived in the Carlyles' house. By the time she had read this far in the letters, she had come to think of Jane and Thomas Carlyle as the eternal owners of the house, permanent residents who had simply gone on vacation, to a different time. Charlotte, too, soon became real to her as she imagined the girl going about from one floor to another, carrying out her duties. Then the day came when, by a coincidence of mind and matter, there were four women in Carlyle's house: Muriel and Jane and Charlotte and, lastly, Elizabeth. That was the day Muriel played the trick.

If there were four women in the Chelsea row house that day, Elizabeth had the least claim to be there. Elizabeth was only a tourist, an unfashionable thing to be, she knew. Yet she had read *Sartor Resartus* and loved it. She had memorized lines. She knew little about Thomas Carlyle's other work or his life, however, and nothing about Jane. She hadn't looked forward to visiting Carlyle's house; it was only something to do in London, where she didn't want to be. She'd been washed ashore in England, after travelling for months through Europe with her boyfriend. They had broken up in Berne one chilly day when all the natives bustled past her with the collars of their trench coats turned up, like spies who knew about her failure to be loved. She had drifted to England because she couldn't be alone in a foreign language. She wanted to go home but they weren't expecting her for weeks and would ask questions if she came back early.

At the beginning, Muriel wasn't at all interested in Elizabeth, as the object of a trick or anything else. She regarded her as just another tourist at the door, a stray tourist on a day when rain had left the stone paving slick, the brick walls dense, the sky pearled and Carlyle's house relatively empty, which was a good thing because Muriel wasn't feeling well. Her body had been taken over by some new swift influenza virus or perhaps she was experiencing sympathetic intestinal symptoms from living in the Carlyles' house and reading of their complaints. Whatever the cause, her illness was not severe enough to have justified closing the house before the official hour.

She opened the door to Elizabeth, who hadn't known if she should knock but had done so quietly, in case. To keep her mind off her stomach cramps, Muriel had been writing what she hoped would become an article about Jane and Charlotte. She hadn't ever written an article before but the relationship had inspired her and she thought it might sell, not to a scholarly journal, but to a certain kind of women's magazine. She had just written a sentence that put Charlotte knocking at the door of Number Five, Cheyne Row, about to be interviewed for the job as maid-of-all-work, when she had to put her pen down to answer Elizabeth's tap, tap, tap. As she opened the door, she was thinking a sentence in which Charlotte, too afraid to look Jane directly in the eye, looked past her, down the hall to the open back door and the garden beyond. And it happened that Elizabeth felt a bit shy, not knowing what sort of protocol might be expected by the small, refined-looking woman who had answered the door. She looked past Muriel instead of looking right at her. The back door was open to relieve some of the oppression of a gloomy day; Elizabeth saw a long rectangle of garden and leaves hanging opaque and heavy from their branches. The branches gave a shudder while she stood there, and splashed drops of water down.

She stepped into the dim wainscotted light of the hall, blinking as her eyes adjusted. Muriel, looking elegant but distracted, asked her to please come in. She explained that she was a mere temporary caretaker, replacing the curator and his wife who'd gone on holidays, but she would answer any questions she could. Meanwhile, her stomach gurgled. It gurgled low and occasionally it gurgled high. Once it squealed, a thin, sharp squeal that rose and turned back on itself so that Elizabeth had a quick, uncomfortable picture in her mind of a length of Muriel's bowel, twisted and looped, through which a bubble of gas was whistling along like a mouse through a hungry boa constrictor. Both Muriel and Elizabeth pretended the intestinal effusions weren't happening, although once or twice Muriel unconsciously stepped back from the sounds to dissociate herself from their source.

"I'm afraid I shall have to ask you to go through the house on your own," Muriel said. "I shall have to stay near the door to welcome other guests."

It was just what Elizabeth wanted to hear.

Muriel went back to her article, which was to be an imaginative reconstruction of young Charlotte's experiences as the London maid-of-all-work in the house of a great man. She was not planning to write a chronological account but to discuss Charlotte's occupation there in terms of things – specifically things owned by Thomas Carlyle that Charlotte would have used or handled. Muriel had two good reasons for this approach. First, the Victorians hadloved things; there was no more happily cluttered age. Second, in her own time in Carlyle's house, Muriel had observed all kinds of visitors involved in the same pursuit. They fastened on things. What else was there for them to see in an abandoned house, after all? They often said, more to themselves than to her, "So that's his hat … his chair … his desk … his pipe … his this … his that…." as if one of these things or an accumulation of them might possibly give up what they all had come for, what they all wanted to possess and take home: a souvenir shred of his genius. Often these were people who hadn't read any of his books and probably wouldn't have liked them, but they knew that he had been famous and that his name meant something still, although they weren't sure what it was. She had seen greed in their eyes. She had seen their belief in the power of things, their superstitious desire to have the unattainable made concrete. They would have eaten his heart and brains, given the chance. She could see them weighing the risk of being told off for putting his hat (hanging there on its peg at the back door as it did in his lifetime) on their own heads. For picking up his pen and trotting off home to write a fluent novel. For sticking his pipe stem between their own lips and inhaling his spirit. Shamefully, she had performed these actions herself.

She was calling her article "Carlyle's House," and she had a subtitle: "In Which We See Charlotte Southam in the Midst of Things," which she thought set the right tone. She meant to create a kaleidoscope of things with Charlotte in the centre, more or less juggling them all. Her first sentence was not what she would have wished. She wrote: "How she got her foot in the door even she couldn't remember in later years." Since she had suggested herself for the position of caretaker and still couldn't believe she'd had the nerve, Muriel feared she was, with very little disguise, writing about herself. Nevertheless, she persevered, angling off into the facts of little Charlotte's life, which (she was grateful to remember) had nothing to do with her own.

"She thought her mother must have arranged for the interview," Muriel wrote, "her mother who was not really her mother but her aunt, for Charlotte was that quintessential Victorian heroine, an orphan."

Little Charlotte's orphanhood was a fact, but Muriel feared the sentence promised the kind of story she wasn't likely to deliver. She continued: "Unfortunately, she was not a romantic orphan. The aunt and uncle who raised her were sufficiently poor to help her qualify as a figure of romance, but they were too good to oppress her. Also, her mother and father had left her no legacy, hidden or otherwise, no ancient name, no blood ties, and worst of all, no hoard of things to make her interesting." At last she had reached the things she had meant to write about, but there was more to say about Charlotte. "She was a Cockney girl of the working class and she wasn't a bit pathetic. Still, she appreciated the value of things (Muriel was determined to stay on track) and knew that her lack of them was the cause of her having to work for a living. She didn't let it get her down. Her aunt, an energetic woman she called Mother, had often commended Charlotte on her capacity for enjoying life, often enough that Charlotte had come to believe she did have that helpful aptitude, and acted accordingly. Thus she had discovered early in life (she was orphaned at the age of four) that she could delight in other people's things without the cost or the bother of ownership."

Muriel looked around the sitting room that had been restored to seem as if it and its furnishings hadn't changed in more than a hundred years. She appreciated her short tenure among these things. She remembered the first time she visited the tall brick row house on the famous street in Chelsea near the Thames. As soon as she had stepped over the threshold, she had wished she could live in its dark narrow rooms.

Charlotte had first walked up the white steps to the front door one day in June. 1858. She was fifteen. She would have looked small on that doorstep. "Surrounded by the white frame and lintel, topped by an iron lantern half her size...."

This was the sentence Muriel had reached when she put down her pen and went to the door so that Elizabeth could walk in and look past her down the hall to the green garden and the swag of grey sky that had fallen between the brick walls. And her stomach was acting up. It was embarrassing but she was thinking about her next sentence and that helped to distance her. The young woman had looked pleased to be given free rein of the house. Technically, Muriel should have confiscated her knapsack but she seldom did that, certainly not for a young woman on her own, who was dressed in clean jeans and had washed her hair recently.

She went back to her article and wrote: "The next day Charlotte was mistress of the garden, as soon as she was out in it alone, mistress of the flagstone patio, the pretty green china stools (which she described to her mother as exquisite – she had seen nothing like them in a garden before), mistress of the pots of geraniums (although she had seen a good many of them before), of the high brick walls and the gravel paths with their borders of box kept six inches high, mistress of the flower beds and the fruit trees, the grape vines, the turnips and the beans, the grass and the big old sheltering walnut tree, and mistress of the earth closet where she sat, knocking her heels against the boards longer than she should have. She didn't notice details; she wasn't the naming kind and barely distinguished the roses from the marigolds. She couldn't have identified Jane's Scottish nettle and gooseberry, brought home from her parents' graves; they were all so much green to Charlotte. But they were her green, as much as they were Jane's or Tom's or the part-time gardener's, because she had got the job.

"On her way to the back steps she saw something sticking out of a chink in the brick wall to her left, just at her eye level. She slid it out. A clay pipe filled with tobacco. She cradled the bowl in her palm, where it fit as if it belonged. And on a hook at the back door, at the head of the stairs to the basement, was a famous hat. She removed the hat from its peg and plopped it on her head. She ducked into the pantry and grinned into the glass of a china cabinet. The hat was two feet wide and made of white straw." Muriel smiled, remembering – as if she had witnessed it – Jane's embarrassment over those hats of Tom's. They were such giant hats, and being white attracted so much attention, that she made him promise not to wear them when she was with him.

Muriel was happy with Charlotte for liking things for themselves rather than for what they represented. At last she had discovered an innocent in Carlyle's house. Her stomach gurgled like a drainpipe. She reminded herself it would not have been all sweetness and light, and wrote: "The kitchen in the cellar was her proper sphere. There, by the light of the fire and one candle, in semi-darkness even on sunny days (of which there were not many in London with its fog), she learned to make the meals Jane and Thomas liked (these were not the same meals), to wash dishes, scrub the counters, black the range and sweep the stone floors to Mrs. Carlyle's satisfaction. There she slept every night and she considered it her domain."

Floor boards creaked over Muriel's head as Elizabeth walked across the room above and ascended another flight of stairs. Rain was hitting the windows gently, like a friend tapping your shoulder, Muriel thought, but it would have been a many-fingered friend, with all those drops. She whisked the simile from her mind and was grateful to be confining herself, in her writing, to facts.

"Although it was her domain," she continued, "the kitchen did not contain much that Charlotte marvelled at. For pure enjoyment, she preferred her less legitimate possession of the furniture and articles she handled in the rest of the house. Lighting fires, opening curtains, cleaning and blacking grates, sweeping and dusting and polishing, airing the bedrooms, turning the mattresses, making the beds, mopping, carrying and emptying, tidying, folding, and mending (housework is child's play with my new little maid, Jane said), everything she touched became hers, but especially the many photographs. For these, she wanted names and got them. "Now, who's this particularly brilliant fellow?" she asked, and Jane laughed and told her it was Alfred Tennyson. Then went away and wrote the question in her notebook, for Jane collected the sayings and witticisms of her maids and it had been some time since she'd been given any she liked. And Charlotte memorized his face. For when he came to call. She had already met Thackeray; his children called her Charley.

"Of all the things in a house cluttered with things, the single one she liked best was the screen that Jane had constructed years before, that sat in the dining room, five feet high with four leaves pasted with prints and drawings and portraits by and of the Carlyles' friends. "I look on it as *your* book, ma'am," she told Jane and shocked that lady into silence. It was a witticism perhaps too astute to be recorded; if on that screen was all that Jane had collected, all she had to show for the years – years in which her husband ate up knowledge and regurgitated it in print – perhaps it wasn't enough."

Of course it hadn't been enough. That was obvious from the letters and the two brief, abandoned journals. Jane had tried to convince herself, and others, that making a good loaf of bread, when her heart and soul went into it, was as important and honourable as making a sculpture ("...it is not the greatness or littleness of 'the duty nearest hand,' but the spirit in which one does it, that makes one's doing noble or mean.") But she had been quoting her husband and she hadn't believed it. An ambitious, energetic woman, she had created nothing that lasted longer than bread. She had kept house, she had made conversation, she had collected friends and lost them.

Muriel felt a presence in the room. She sat very still, staring straight ahead, believing that the presence was Jane, that Jane sat with her, in one of the two corners of the room that were just outside her field of vision. She listened hard. She heard nothing. The rain had stopped. The feeling that Jane was with her left, as if it had never been. She realized that she couldn't hear Elizabeth, who had been upstairs a long time. Probably she was in the study, Muriel decided, mooning over the great man's possessions. An ambivalent expression came to her face, not wholly unconsciously. There was disdain in it, and irritation and sarcasm, but those emotions were mixed with a wiser brand of amusement and even sympathy. She felt her face expressed this although she sat alone. She wasn't at all sure she wasn't trying to communicate or wasn't being communicated with. She sighed (it sounded theatrical and meant to communicate as well – but she really was alone in the room). She picked up her pen.

"As for the great man's things," she wrote, "most of them were kept in his attic study, which Charlotte was not to enter unless called there by himself for the purpose of fetching some book or letter or bit of refreshment he might require. She was to leave the door closed during his absence. Nevertheless, the time came, early in her tenure, when the Carlyles went to Scotland, leaving her in charge of the house. Her mother came in nights to sleep with her and kept her working as steadily as possible during the days. But she couldn't always be there; she had duties of her own. There were long hours when the house belonged to Charlotte. The study door wasn't locked.

She entered at her first opportunity. She sat in his chair, looked out his windows, put her hands all over his desk. She fingered his inkstand and tried a couple of his pens. He had taken his notes and his manuscript on Frederick the Great to work on while he was away, but piles of research material remained. She had no desire to touch his papers, no need to make those words, which were mere facts, her own. She wanted only to investigate, to enjoy herself, to become familiar with his things, but when she left she wanted more."

Muriel looked at the words she had written. She didn't know what she was talking about. What more did Charlotte want? She set her notebook and her pen down and without really thinking about what she was doing or why, she began climbing the three flights to Thomas Carlyle's rooftop study. She climbed slowly because the stairs were steep. She climbed quietly, without considering why she did so.

In the study doorway she paused. Elizabeth had fallen asleep. Sitting in his chair, her hands on his desk, she was sleeping with her chin on her chest. Muriel moved her right foot forward and nearly stepped into the room, but she hesitated with that foot in mid-air, and lowered it quietly. She had noticed that a notebook lay open on the desk.

Quietly, she crossed the room.

Elizabeth had written: "All that men have thought, dreamed, done, and been: the whole External universe and what it holds is but Clothing." It was a quote from *Sartor Resartus*. Muriel would have liked to have picked up the pen and written other, more appropriate lines beneath it: "Well at ease are the Sleepers for whom Existence is but a shallow Dream. But what of the awestruck Wakeful who find it a Reality?" She had found the lines amusing after learning that Carlyle was an insomniac. Her favourite quote, however, came from knowing about his chronic indigestion: "Soul is *not* synonymous with Stomach."

She might have been amused at finding a young tourist sleeping in his chair, after the exertion of writing a couple of dozen words and those not her own. Perhaps another day she would have been. She wasn't amused. She looked down on the bent head, the open arms, and would have liked to slap the girl silly.

She plucked one of the old pens from the stand on the desk. She slipped it into Elizabeth's knapsack and glided out of the room.

When she reached the ground floor, she locked the front door; it was almost closing time anyway. Then she returned to her article. She was not pleased to see where she'd left off, with little Charlotte suddenly, after sitting at the great man's desk, wanting more. Muriel still couldn't decide what it was Charlotte wanted. She certainly did not want to write an article in which it turned out that the fifteen-year-old maid, like every other foolish person who entered the house, wanted to be a great writer. There were two other options. Sitting there, at his desk, the girl might have conjured his physical presence and renewed and fanned a trembling little lick of candle-flame desire, imagining herself on his lap. Muriel hoped it wasn't that. The other possibility, the only one Muriel could approve, was that the girl had found a letter of Tom's to Jane or Jane's to Tom. And her snooping had gotten her thinking along a track that would have been too daring for her to invent. It would have been a letter of Jane's – Tom would have been more careful; it was Jane who had the enthusiasms.

Muriel leafed through the volumes of letters to July 30, 1858, to a letter Jane wrote to Tom before leaving Charlotte in charge of the house, and read: "I have no wish to change Charlotte for an older woman; as she has strength and sense enough for the place, I don't see what I should gain by changing her. She is a *very* good housemaid, and is already a better cook than Ann was. Above all, she is my *servant*, – does what I order, at the first word, – and not my Mistress! For the satisfaction of your imagination, you will find her much bigger and older-looking when you return." Muriel didn't think there was much in that to inspire Charlotte, to encourage her. Another letter, written in September, advised Charlotte: "It will be a great shame to you, if you have not the house perfectly sorted when we return – having for so long had no family to attend to…." In October's letters Muriel found what she was looking for: "She is quite a jewel of a servant. Far more like an adopted child than a London maid-of-all-work." If Jane had written so in October, on her return from Scotland, the coals for that warm thought must have been heaped in June and July, when she'd taught Charlotte how to keep her house and the girl's quickness and good humour had made housekeeping seem like play. Perhaps she had written words to that effect in the summer and Charlotte, idly turning pages (oh, not quite idly – looking for references to herself, surely, especially at age fifteen), found: "almost like a daughter" and "more like an adopted child." And wouldn't she think, then, that there was a chance for her to become just that? This was the option Muriel much preferred, although it wasn't quite the way she'd first seen the relationship between the Carlyles and their little maid. The exploitation wasn't so one-sided. If Charlotte wanted to be more to them than servant, and worked to make them love her, wasn't her innocence lost?

At any rate, Charlotte's desires shouldn't enter into the article; it was the readers' desires Muriel wanted to pique and play with, the readers who hadn't made it to Chelsea or the other heritage homes of the famous or who had gone but hadn't dared to put hats on their heads or pens in their knapsacks. She wanted to write about things, about facts not feelings, just as Tom had advised Jane to do in her letters and journals. But she had not written about things the way she had hoped to do, spinning them around a central Charlotte, examining them as they turned for the benefit of her readers, feeding their lust to know that in some facet of some thing or from some glitter as the light caught some facet, the secret of genius could be discerned. She hadn't written of things at all like that. She might as well give up.

Muriel stared into space until, with no conscious effort, almost as if it had been given, she thought of a new subtitle. She picked up her pen and wrote it down: "In which We See Charlotte Southam in the Midst of Sensations." She continued, feeling fresh. "The first time Charlotte stood at the front door to Number Five, Cheyne Row, she felt some trepidation. She feared the Carlyles might decide she was too small, too slow, or too muddled or they might decide they disliked her. That didn't last; it went away, in time, as her confidence in her ability to please increased – until that day in the study. After that day in the study, when she discovered herself not content with her lot but wanting more, each time she let herself into the house, her heart beat faster. She felt that way only while standing on the doorstep; once inside she was home free, but on the doorstep, with the key in her fingers, the lantern above her was always about to fall."

Muriel paused. She was writing about herself again, about her own ambitions, which she should have long ago given up. However, she decided it wasn't obvious. She stood, in her imagination as she often had in fact, outside the door, the lantern above her, the key in her hand, and wrote: "Charlotte wanted too much. The man she called Father said, 'Don't forget your place, girl,' and she forgot it every day."

"She forgot her place and that meant she was not always the best of servants, even with Jane's prodding and her mother's supervision. With all she had to do, those days the Carlyles were in Scotland, she often sat at windows looking dreamily at the streets outside. She sat with Nero, Jane's black and white dog on her lap and imagined that she, too, was theirs.

"Then Tom was coming home, unexpectedly, before Jane. A long letter, panic-jammed and not just between the lines, arrived from Jane to prepare her for his (predicted) calamitous return. 'Trouble him with as few questions as possible.... I think you can now cook most of the things he takes oftenest, boiled fowl, mutton broth, chops and bread and ground rice puddings – if you take pains to please him I have no doubt you will. And if he look fussed and *cross*, never mind, so long as you are doing your best, travelling always puts him in a fever... Heaven help you and him well thro it!.... Take care your kitchen is in order – when he goes to light his pipe – He will see.'

"Then he was back, he was in her kitchen, lighting his pipe before her fire where he took his last pipe of each day when he was at home. (He didn't like to smoke where it would disturb Jane.) With only the fire lighting him and with smoke clouding his head, like a volcano he sat meditating in her kitchen while she waited in the back room with her candle, sleepily, because he kept her from her bed. She waited with no thoughts in her mind, her body tired out, relieved that her kitchen and the house in general had passed whatever inspection his pale eyes had subjected it to. Almost companionably, she waited, for he sat tired too, returned from his long walks through the dark city streets.

"She couldn't wake up in the mornings in time to have his breakfast ready. Every morning until Jane came home, he came to the head of the basement stairs and banged the dining room poker against the wall. She rushed to dress and make his tea and porridge, served them to him breathless and too afraid to apologize. He said nothing about it.

"Then Jane was home and she was *pleased*! Pleased with the cover Charlotte had crocheted for the living room sofa. Pleased with the jet-black kitten Charlotte had acquired the day after she'd discovered mice in the pantry. Pleased with the housework. All her life, Charlotte would remember that wonderful first evening when she followed Jane with her bags up to her room to show Jane her red bed shining, the room shining, and knew that Jane was *pleased* with her. When afterwards she remembered that moment, the bedroom all in order and Jane smiling, her black eyes approving every detail, it came back to her with its antecedent superimposed – with the bed apart, the smell of beeswax and soap, the furniture covered in sheets, and all the feathers out of the mattresses and pillows, airing on the floor. She had herself and, instead of her mother, Jane, soberly dressed in black, up to their boot tops in drifting feathers, and feathers in the air and the smallest and tenderest of feathers caught on their sleeves and in their collars and in their hair – she had that picture, that memory of their happiness at her virtue, at her mistress's appreciation.

"The next morning she said to Jane, while pouring her tea, 'Scotland must be a fresh, airy place. I should like to go there. You did smell so beautiful when you came in at the door last night!'"

Muriel breathed in. Past the sharp, almost sweet smell of old wood and damp stone, was the smell of the garden, wet grass and earth, and past that was the smell of exhaust and the mingled chemicals of the city's pollution. She was not very satisfied by her writing about sensations. She should have employed a stream of consciousness technique, tried to capture the ebb and flow of an ocean of sensation. She had been too concerned that in describing the atmosphere Charlotte lived in, or in attempting her responses to the atmosphere, she would have seemed to be trying to reconstruct that long-gone world in order to inhabit it herself. Wasn't a certain distance, and objectivity – wasn't objectivity necessary? A sound from the attic study, of a chair being pushed back, made her start. Incredibly, she had forgotten the young woman who had fallen asleep at the desk. She had forgotten her illness as well. She sat still, she felt for it, for the fullness, the sinking feeling, the cramps, she sent her mind floating down her middle, seeking trouble; she felt nothing specific but she didn't feel quite well either. On the road to recovery, she decided. The young woman was descending flight after flight and soon would be upon her.

Elizabeth tried to step quietly, but not too quietly, down the stairs. She didn't wish to appear apologetic in case her long stay in the attic study hadn't been noticed. She wasn't sure how long she'd been asleep, but knew it was a few minutes past closing time. She hoped the caretaker had forgotten she was in the house, she hoped the woman had gone into the private apartment on the third floor so she could avoid her altogether and sneak out of the house. From the foot of the stairs to the front door was an open stretch that would take only seconds to cross. It would be a relief to get out of the house unnoticed. She imagined herself outside, on the streets and at Victoria Station, anonymous, with people rushing past her.

The woman was waiting for her, standing by the door. She was such a fastidious-looking little woman, restraint in her posture and in every gesture, that Elizabeth almost believed she must have imagined the earlier noisy workings of her intestines. She did look pale. Elizabeth wondered if she should ask her how she was, yet it seemed it would be an infringement to allude to her illness, she stood so upright and bravely elegant with her arm outstretched to guide Elizabeth toward the door.

When Muriel had slipped the pen into Elizabeth's knapsack, she had acted on a moment's inspiration. She'd had a mad idea that she would ask the girl to empty the bag before she left the house. Whereupon the pen would be discovered and who knew what depths of embarrassment would be revealed. But she had known even when she'd picked up the pen that she would never carry out such a plan. It was too audacious a trick for her to pull off. She wasn't a good enough actor. It was also (maybe) too mean. Muriel wasn't convinced of that. Wouldn't the discovery of Carlyle's pen, on its way out of the house, simply put into concrete form the girl's presumptions and pretensions? Wasn't it an action taken for the girl's own good? Not that it mattered now. She had thought of a better idea, not so daring or confrontational, but more interesting ultimately. She would let the girl leave, taking the pen with her. She would imagine the pen riding in the knapsack on the tube, in Harrods, at the Tower, probably through Dickens's house. She would imagine the moment the girl rifled through her bag, looking for a pen, and pulled it out. Wouldn't it be interesting to imagine her moral dilemma? And to see if she returned it?

While she stood at the door, trying to smile, a queer, intense pain gripped her bowels and subverted her intentions. She nearly gasped at the shock of the pain. She had to steel herself to continue standing straight.

Elizabeth couldn't tell at first whether the caretaker was smiling or grimacing in pain. Then Muriel's eyes opened so wide they seemed to bulge and at the same time her forehead and her upper lip glistened with perspiration. Although Elizabeth still felt reticent about approaching the subject of the woman's health, she thought it might be wrong to leave her alone.

"I'm afraid I stayed past closing time," she said. "I'm sorry."

"Not at all," Muriel said. A look almost of horror tightened her features. "You haven't inconvenienced me," she went on. Her face now had tightened to the degree she had to speak through clenched teeth, but she continued. "I forgot the time myself."

"Is anything wrong?" Elizabeth asked. She couldn't help but be alarmed and tried to think if she knew how to call an ambulance in London.

"No, no," Muriel said. "A little indigestion. I shall lie down now." She said it firmly, opening the door as she spoke.

Elizabeth, dismissed, made her way down the rain-glazed steps. The door closed behind her. She walked slowly at first, past the iron railings, and looked back up at the house in case the woman had changed her mind and wanted help. The door stayed closed and no one came to the windows. Elizabeth began to hurry away. It was only late afternoon but the sky was unnaturally dark. The slate sidewalks were wet enough that water splashed out from under her running shoes. Off Cheyne Row there was traffic, there were several other pedestrians, and she wished she knew one of them. She had no one to tell about the incident of the odd caretaker at Carlyle's House. She was sure if she could tell someone about it over a beer in a pub it could become a funny story and prove her anxiety groundless.

She tried to put the woman behind her, to think about Carlyle, instead, and consider her experience in his house. She had felt appropriately humble in the attic; she had been amazed that she could sit in his chair, at his desk. She tried to recreate that moment, when she had settled into his chair, her hands on his desk, looking out his study window. The window frame, but not the view, appeared to her. The caretaker's face, taut with fear, was what she saw. But there was nothing she could do. The woman had clearly wanted her to go. Obediently, she hurried through the drenched and nearly empty side streets of Chelsea with a new certainty that, however much she hurried, she had no place to go. Her throat began to sting. Tears threatened. She decided she hated the prim little front gardens she was passing, with their tasteful geometric patterns in brick, she hated white stone, polished doorknobs and all signs of middle-class domesticity, and would die before she lived in a house with a window box. Then she remembered, as if she had forgotten it, that she had fallen asleep in Carlyle's house. Like Goldilocks in the bears' den. It might have been the oddest thing she'd ever done.

But before that, sitting at his desk, she had thought of the quotation. She had pulled out her notebook and pen from her knapsack, and had written from memory, pleased with herself for remembering.

"All that men have thought, dreamed, done, and been: the whole External universe and what it holds is but Clothing." As she walked along, hemmed in by the city, the quotation eased her mind; it made her think of the ocean, of space. But, she thought, if the ocean and space were, like everything else, merely clothing, then there must be something beating beyond them, untouchable – something that could not fail. The rhythm of her thoughts, as much as the content, soothed her. She was recapturing the feeling she'd had in the study when she'd been lulled to sleep. Now, for some reason, maybe because she was trying to make the phrase her own, she substituted the word "women" for the word "men" and found it didn't work. She couldn't believe in it. What women thought, dreamed and did meant something, at least to themselves. Meant something to each other, too. She thought of the caretaker; their brief meeting had significance, or it might have had. She decided the problem with Carlyle's idea was the word "men". He used it in the abstract and people were not abstract, it was ridiculous to think of them that way. She felt sorry for men, for centuries semantically absorbed into grand concepts. She began to walk faster, enjoying these thoughts on the way to the King's Road. The pain in her throat from wanting to cry lessened and became a fullness; she was full of tears still, but it was not an unpleasant fullness. She began to think in a vague way of the more melancholy English poets with their solemn enjoyment of their own sadness. The idea of a vast heart beating in the great beyond seemed superfluous now. She almost smiled, thinking a stroll through a graveyard would be the perfect thing, in this dim light.

Muriel had doubled over as soon as she had shut the door and locked it. The pain was so intense she imagined herself crawling to the sofa; she didn't think she'd be able to straighten up again. She wondered if she had eaten something that had poisoned her. Soon she was sick enough she would have considered death a cure.

She spent the hours until night came dragging herself from the bathroom to the sofa and back again, until her body had purged itself, finally, and lay itself down, for the last time, on the sofa. She was too weak to climb the stairs, too exhausted to sleep. She lay in fetal position on the sofa, robbed of all resources.

She must have fallen asleep eventually because she was wakened by a bossy banging at the door. Disoriented, she tried to rise from the sofa but fell back. The banging resumed. She lifted her arm weakly, to fend it off. She heard footsteps retreating and consulted her watch. It was hours past opening time; she'd known it would be. The day was bright, for London, and she had a sense, from the back of the house, of a breeze. She hadn't thought to close the door to the garden, and now was grateful for the freshness coming in. She thought of Jane, who had passed many bad nights in this house. She closed her eyes and imagined Jane lying on the sofa after a mostly sleepless night. The back door was open, the garden breathed its freshness into the house and a new little maid bustled in the kitchen, not at top efficiency, but cheerfully. Jane, like Muriel, had never had a child, but she had at least had a servant in the house. She hadn't spent hours sick and alone.

Preferring action to self-pity, Muriel dragged herself up the stairs to the modernized apartment the curator and his wife had left in immaculate order. She plugged in the kettle to make herself tea and ran a bath. She had kept the apartment the way she had found it and now regretted all the mess she might have made. She stood over the kettle until it boiled, thinking of the possibility of leaving the tub to run over. Of course she was living in the house, looking after it, precisely because she was known to be the sort of person who would not do that sort of thing. She no longer felt unwell, only limp and resigned. She had never been a fan of resignation, she thought while wetting her tea bag. The thought arrested her. She didn't overpour the pot but she imagined herself doing so; she pictured the boiling water gushing over the teapot, over the counter, to the floor, to her feet, scalding her feet. Carefully, she put the kettle down. She set the lid in place on the pot and drew the cosy down. If she didn't like resignation, what had she been doing playing that trick on that young woman? That trick designed to teach her to resign herself to her place in life.

She didn't know how many visitors turned away from the house that day; she left the door locked and kept to her apartment. In the early evening, after a nap and a light supper from a can of chicken soup, she went downstairs again and resumed work on her article. She'd decided on a new subtitle: "In Which We See Charlotte Southam in the Midst of Patterns."

She began: "It is June, 1858. The sky has rained; the London streets retain that impression. A middle-aged couple, old friends of the Carlyles named David Aitken and Bess, are approaching the door to Number Five, Cheyne Row. On the other side of that door, Jane Carlyle and her new little maid, Charlotte, are putting their heads together. They are kneeling at the door, examining the action of one of the latchkeys that hasn't been operating properly. They are trading lively suggestions like two London sparrows turning beetles over for one another."

After these two words, "one" and "another," Muriel threw her pen – straight across the room. It hit the wainscotting and clattered to the floor. She was starting off all wrong – again. Two sparrows indeed. There was, in fact, a sparrow in the house at the time, and not a very lively specimen. Jane had rescued it from some boys who'd been trying to kill it. The poor thing had a broken or dislocated wing and who knew what else wrong with it. She and Charlotte kept it in a box and fed and watered it. Jane had experience nursing a bird, her canary had been sick for months. What had she said about it? "The canary continues to tumble off its perch, and I to lift it up! What a blessing to have somebody to always lift one up when one falls off the perch!"

Muriel retrieved her pen. She would simply have to write it as she saw it. And heard it. Although she hadn't heard the ideas Jane and Charlotte had exchanged when she'd pictured them bending together peering at the key that wouldn't turn in the lock, she had heard their frivolous bantering tone, she had heard affection in their two voices.

She was unable to begin, her pen was immobilized again. Two women, a lock, a key that wouldn't work. A Freudian scene. But what did it mean? For a few seconds, she really was stopped and didn't see how she could go on, it was so clear she didn't know what she was writing about. But then she remembered it was fact she was recording; the incident had happened, it was history. And then, too, she remembered what Jane had said on beginning her journal and that gave her courage. She would write as Jane had: "...quite promiscuously without any moral end in view, but just as the Scotch professor drank whiskey, because I like it, and because it's cheap."

She continued: "Bess Aitken hustles along the sidewalk, holding her skirts above the wet. David follows, watching the water sprinkle out from under her heels. Up the steps they go. Bess raises her knuckles to knock just as the key turns in the lock and the door swings open. Bess nearly falls into the house. Stunned, all three straighten themselves."

"'Is this Mrs. Carlyle's?' Bess asks Jane.

"'My goodness!' Jane cries. ' Unrecognized. At my own door!'

"At the sound of her voice, Bess knows her. She staggers back; David takes her elbow but isn't quick enough to stop her saying, 'God preserve me, Jane! That you?'

"It has been only a few years since Bess saw Jane, but they have been years of illness and, worse, of jealousy, and they have come to this: all Jane's youth and looks are gone. Bess flaps and blusters and shakes her umbrella, scattering raindrops on them all before David takes Jane's arm as well as hers and guides them both into the house. Charlotte stands back, watching, too sorry for her mistress to be amused but knowing (because she is fifteen) this will never happen to her."

Muriel stopped there and went to bed. She thought this approach was going to work. She would describe the patterns simply, write them out and not think about them.

The next day she opened the house and, her gracious self again, played hostess to several tourists and three students who actually knew a thing or two about Carlyle. Between visitors, she added to her article, determined to keep to her decision. She didn't like her mind to idle on its contents, even for a few minutes, because it was likely to remind her of the young woman she'd tricked and make her feel guilty.

She wrote: "Events combined to relieve Jane Carlyle's wretchedness in 1858 and both her physical and mental health improved temporarily. Carlyle still toiled on the mountain that was Frederick, but the first two volumes had been published – to acclaim – making it seem possible that he would one day reach the end. Another event that helped her was the death of her rival for her husband's affections and esteem – Lady Harriet Ashburton. This was an event so important to her and so blindly and blithely unacknowledged by her husband that he could write, in his introduction to a group of her letters from the summer of 1857, an obituary paragraph on Lady Harriet and follow it immediately with a paragraph that started: 'My Jane's miserable illness now over, a visit to Haddington was steadily in view all summer.' Her illness did abate slowly but her jealousy was not as easily soothed. It erupted in various directions and burned friends left and right. Before Charlotte was hired, it had found a major outlet in the person of the previous maid, Ann, who'd been left housekeeping for Carlyle while Jane travelled to Scotland. During her travels, Tom had fallen ill and Jane had wanted to turn homeward, had wanted to feel needed, and was told (or read between the lines of letters) that she was not. Ann had been with the Carlyles five years but the relationship couldn't survive once Jane suspected she aspired to be a rival. In February, 1858, Ann left, with relief, no doubt, on both sides. In June, after a couple of failures, Jane hired Charlotte Southam, which became one of the better happenings of those years. Her letters are full of regard for the girl: 'She is a perfect jewel, that young girl....' 'I find all extremely right here. A perfectly-cleaned house, and a little maid, radiant with "virtue is its own reward...."' 'My little Charlotte continues to behave like the good girl of a Fairy Tale!' '...Mr. Carlyle is hard at work as usual; and the house would be dull enough, if it were not for the plenty of people, – often more than enough – who come to see me in the forenoons, and for Charlotte's dancing spirits and face radiant with good humour and kindliness all day long. And the strange little being has so much good sense and reflection in her, that she is quite as good to talk with as most of the fine ladies that come about me.'

"What is the reward for the good girl of a fairy tale? She gets taken to Scotland with the Carlyles. Summer of 1859.

"What is the pattern in Scotland? Life in a garden. Sun and sea and pure air – the pure air of rural Fife. Instead of the heat of London and the smell of the river – coolness and the smell of roses."

Now was supposed to follow a scene, similar to the scene at the front door, that placed the players in the garden setting and showed, through one example, the pattern of those days. Unfortunately, Muriel had never been to Scotland. She supposed she could describe Charlotte strolling down any country lane, dallying with village youths who admired her because she was new in town, quick to make friends and it didn't hurt that she was attractive. She could have Tom dash into any ocean and frolic there like a teenager, only to become ill and feel like an old man. She supposed she did not have to have any special knowledge of Scotland to know how Jane felt, watching them, exhausted after her journey and ill again, to know why she said: "Decidedly there is everything here needed for happiness, but just *one* thing – the faculty of being happy! And *that*, unfortunately, I had never much of in my best days; and in the days that are, it is lost to me altogether."

The problem was, Muriel did not want to bring this pattern to life. The thought of it depressed her. In Scotland, Charlotte had become "the happiest of girls" and Jane the most miserable of women. She had brought Charlotte along to treat her and perhaps, although she wouldn't have admitted it, to indulge herself in pretending they were a family. The desire for a child had not left her. In her first year of marriage, she had sewed a baby's layette that had never been used. When the second Lady Ashburton (a woman Jane liked much better than the first) was expecting her first child, Jane dreamed she was searching for a crying baby and could not find it. Yet it was too late for her to adopt a daughter, especially when the child in question was a servant and especially when her own attitude toward the girl was becoming increasingly ambivalent. Charlotte seemed to be taking her mistress for granted; she would have to be reminded, gently, of her place.

Muriel was sorry she wasn't able to reconstruct those weeks of a sixteen-year-old's summer, before she got reminded of her place. Those weeks when Charlotte must have felt on the edge of achieving her hopes. But Muriel couldn't remember the last time she had experienced hope without immediately squelching it. Even for another person, she wouldn't have been able to sustain it past the length of a sentence. And she was getting tired of her task. She couldn't see the point of continuing. What good would it do anyone to see a pattern repeating itself in Jane Carlyle's life, a pattern in which, having felt jealousy for someone, the woman could never again view the person without its withering effects. So that they went home to Cheyne Row with Jane glad to get things back to normal. And Charlotte continued to bloom into womanhood, Jane continued to be ill, and Tom continued to ignore her and obsess over Frederick. Then Nero, the lap dog, was run over by a cart and began to die by slow degrees and had to be put down after months of decline, which saddened them all. Then Charlotte got prettier and happier in herself and more lax about pleasing, while Jane got sicker and sadder and Tom couldn't sleep at all from worrying that he would never finish his monumental work. And Jane suffered more of her torments of mind. And Charlotte was dismissed.

If the pattern had ended there, it wouldn't have filled Muriel so depressingly with tedium, but it didn't end there. Charlotte, repentant, wanted to come back. Jane, repentant, wanted her back, especially when she got sick again and the servant who'd replaced Charlotte could barely keep up with the housework and had no time for nursing and Charlotte stepped in, not hired but as a friend or daughter would have, to look after Jane. ("She has been much about me and I don't know what I should have done without her, to cook for me, and show me some human kindness when I was ill.... But I am glad at the same time that I had fortitude to resist her tears, and her request to be taken back as cook. I told her some day I might take her back; but she had much to learn and unlearn first. Still it is gratifying to feel that one's kindness to the girl has not been all lost on her, for she really loves both of us passionately – only that passionate loves, not applied to practical uses, are good for so little in this matter-of-fact-world.")

Now – what good would it do anyone, Muriel asked herself, to know that it was not ambition but love that had led the child to wish she could be adopted? Muriel slammed the book of letters closed. She thought of sweeping both volumes off the little table onto the floor but denied herself that melodramatic gesture. What satisfaction did the girl have in seeing that Jane had to hire two servants to accomplish all the work she'd done herself during the time of her desire to please? None. She had no satisfaction from it. She only wanted to be there, to live with them. As for Jane, she said (Muriel grabbed the book of letters and paged irritably though it to find what she was looking for): "Often in the dead of night I am seized with a wild desire to clear the house of these newcomers, and take back my little Charlotte, who is still hanging on at her mother's, in a wild hope that one or other of them, or both, may break down, and she be reinstated in her place."

What good would it do anyone, reading a women's magazine, to know that in November of that same year Charlotte was rehired, her love for Jane and Jane's for her acknowledged? That the perfume of reunion was sweeter than all the roses in Scotland and went to both their heads? That Jane said: "I haven't been as near what they call 'happy' for many a day as in the first flush of little Charlotte! She looked so bursting with ecstasy as she ran up and down the house, taking possession, as it were, of her old work, and as she showed in the visitors (not her business, but she would open the door to them all the first time, to show herself, and receive their congratulations) that it was impossible not to share in her delighted excitement!"

What good would it do anyone to know how pleasant it was for Jane to have Charlotte back, eager to please her, and to know it was too good to last? For of course Charlotte let Jane down. Of course she left; she had her life ahead of her.

Night was falling by the time Muriel had wound down to these thoughts. She went to the back door to lock it and saw how black the trees were against the sky, which never got fully dark because of the city lights. She wished she was out of London. She went to bed without supper; she had no appetite.

The next day Elizabeth came back, early in the morning, at the hour the house was to open. Muriel unlocked the front door and slipped out to feel what kind of day she had in store, and there the girl was, her foot on the first step. (It was a cool day and windy. The wind seemed to have come from a long way off.)

Muriel stepped back and held the door. Elizabeth again entered the dark hallway, then Muriel led the way to the drawing room and indicated a chair the girl could sit on. She'd had a moment's excitement on the doorstep but she couldn't afford to let it continue. She waited silently to hear what the girl would say.

Elizabeth dug into her knapsack, which she had dropped on the floor by her feet. She rummaged in the bag; her long hair fell over her face and hid her. When she held the pen up, she flipped her hair back out of her eyes and looked directly at Muriel. She said, "I found this in my bag."

Muriel said nothing. She was wondering what would happen if she admitted she had put the pen into the girl's bag.

"I didn't take it," Elizabeth said.

Muriel still kept quiet. The girl didn't continue.

"I think you must have," Muriel said.

Elizabeth set the pen on the table beside her chair. She closed her knapsack and stood, slinging it over one shoulder.

"Or do you think it fell in?" Muriel said. "It's not a valuable pen, in any case. It wasn't his, you know. They wouldn't leave his pens lying about for tourists to take."

Elizabeth looked around the room. Because she had wanted to avoid the woman, she had missed this room on her first visit. She had also missed the basement where the kitchen was and she'd had only a glimpse of the garden. She had hoped to view them on this trip, but of course she wouldn't, now. She turned to go.

"You needn't have returned," Muriel said, and closed the door.

Elizabeth walked away. Her indignation made her stride through the streets without seeing but she slowed along the King's Road enough to look into the knowing brown eyes of a young man she'd noticed there before, playing his guitar on the street corner. "Come here often?" he asked and she laughed, then her eyes filled with tears. He took her for a beer. It didn't seem strange to be drinking so early in the morning. He had enough change to buy the first round. She told him about the caretaker at Carlyle's house. He said the interesting thing was, why had she gone back? Was it just because she thought the pen had to be returned? Or had the pen been an excuse? He asked if she had heard of Swedenborg, one of the Victorians' favourite philosophers, who believed that after death we each go to live in the house where we belong. Maybe we are all orphans, he said, looking for that house. He also said she could live with him if she liked for the rest of her stay in London. He was from Toronto and could use someone to share his space. She declined. In her few days in the city, she had come to enjoy her solitary sadness and she could see he would insist on making it universal and destroy it.

After Elizabeth left, Muriel sat very straight, staring ahead. She did not admire reproach. Jane had fallen into it; she had not been able to resist the temptation. Charlotte had gone off to better herself, she had moved to the country, to the sun and fresh air of The Wilderness, the Kent home of the Marquis of Camden, near Sevenoaks. Presumably she had been happy there as under-housemaid. ("Oh child! child! you have no idea of the disappointment, the heart-sorrow you caused me! I had set so much love on you, and so much hope! So much permanent good was to have come out of our chance-relation for both of us!") ("I wish you had never left my house, Dear! I should have been better able to help and console you.... And what opportunities you would have had to help and console *me*!") (And the last letter, a few months before Jane's death: "I have none of the *love* for Jessy I had for *you*! No servant has ever been for me the sort of *adopted* child that *you* were!")

Something nagged at Muriel; she was dissatisfied with the article she'd been attempting but it wasn't that. She was thinking of *Sartor Resartus*, the tailor retailored, that invented biography of a man, his life reconstructed from the scraps of information found in six paper bags. How could one bag the truth? One could only imagine what people said and did, thought and dreamed, and there were so many variables, so many possibilities, including the possibility that none of it mattered, that under the clothes were patterns that could not be seen straight on.

She rose from the sofa and paced up and down. The room felt cold; the wind must be from the east. She thought she remembered one of Dickens's characters locking himself in his room whenever the east wind blew. Poor Jane had felt the cold; she had bitched about it often. She had worn layers of flannel petticoats – blanket flannel – in the winter and wrapped herself in shawls. Muriel stopped pacing. She could almost feel Jane shivering in the corner of the sofa. She went and sat down again, as if beside her.

She thought she would try to master the article over the next few days. Like a stutterer who cannot pronounce certain sounds without halting, she would begin once more. With a new subtitle. She knew what it would be: "At the Door Again." She tried to think what she would include under this heading. She pictured Jane on one side of the door, Charlotte on the other. But there was nothing more to write. There they were, at the door again. That was all.

Acts of Mercy

In a time when the earth was flat.... Or, in a time when art was flat, when red and blue and a great deal of gold puddled luminous and frank on canvas and on tapestry.... When artists were anonymous, when all but popes and kings and queens and the most violent knights were anonymous because all served for the glory of God.... When living was preparing for dying because the Day of Judgement was imminent.... When a ship docked in Messina and brought plague to Italy, after years of internal strife, after economic collapse, an earthquake and famine.... When superstition passed for knowledge because science could not answer the question: why these people suffered.... A man named Lodovico travelled from Firenze to Orvieto.

He strode along the roadside while carts and men on horseback passed him by. Walking through others' dust. But not a humble man. A proud man who had adopted humility as he'd adopted his red cloak and hood, for his own reasons.

So said Isabel, who had conjured him from a sentence in a book. The book was trying to teach her; some of its sentences were more persuasive than others. Lodovico stepped off the page because he was completely garbed in red. He did not come with a name. Isabel gave him that. She gave him the name of an artist whose last name she had forgotten, one of those few artists who had made it to history books. Although she had invented him, Lodovico was more visible in his red from head to toe than anyone on the slow train from Florence to Orvieto.

Of course she talked to herself; there was no one else. In her hotel room she said the name Lodovico, trying for an Italian accent. She stood between the dresser and the bed in the empty room, saying his name and watching the bathroom door in case by will she could make it open and make Lodovico emerge drying his hands on one of the two thin towels.

If she could not imagine him in her room, at least she could see him on the streets of Orvieto. He had a mission that had nothing to do with her, separated as they were by time. Yet his presence, her image of him walking in these narrow streets, had persuaded her to stop here. Also, she was experiencing one of those ironies of travelling. Riding up from the station to the old town on the funicular, she'd been frightened. Her car had ascended faster than anything of antique vintage should be allowed to travel, and at the same time another car had barrelled down. She'd been certain they would crash. Then, when she stepped on firm ground, she felt safe – so safe she took a bed for the night, possibly for several nights, on top of a volcano. The volcano was said to be extinct, but she did not see how anyone could be sure of that.

She went for a walk. Strolling through a bit of green by a small hospital, she came to the edge of the cliffs, where it was possible to walk along the stone wall. The wall was about bench height; she sat and looked at the view and did not once glance over her shoulder. She concentrated on the landscape below, the fields and roads that spilled away from her at such an angle she wondered how people, living here, could ever have thought the world was flat. With the ancient stones beneath her, and with her perspective from on top of all the world she could see, she got the feeling that someone like herself had sat here hundreds of years before, warmed by the sun and safe, in Orvieto. The safe-at-last kind of safe, high on the top of a hill town.

She got up and walked along the edges of the old town, letting the tilting green fields and vineyards of Umbria roll by like scenery in a movie. She put out her hand every once in a while, put it out nonchalantly and knocked the enemy off the wall. One by one they all pitched backwards, and fell with a thud far below.

Back in her room, while she showered, she thought about Lodovico. She would have liked a man in her room, a man of her choosing. She pulled on her clean jeans and a shirt. She had worried about the jeans. Most European women her age looked elegant in fine woven fabrics, in dark colours. She had worried the jeans made her look too American, attracted too much attention. Because she was being followed. She had been followed for weeks, across Italy, and not by a man she had invented. But she would not change the way she dressed. She tugged at the waistband; her jeans were snug, having recently been washed. Within the hour, the denim would stretch to fit her like a second, tougher skin.

She went to the window to look down into the cramped street until something happened. At once (as if her left eye and her right were bringing them together), a small car rounded the tight corner and a woman pushed a child in a stroller toward it. The driver braked hard before the stroller. Isabel realized she hadn't feared for a moment that the child or the woman would be hurt. She had put her trust in the instincts of the driver; she'd assumed he was used to negotiating streets the width of sidewalks.

This was the place to make a stand. It had always been a good place, a city easy to defend from its position three hundred feet above the countryside. However, the book she was reading said invasion from outsiders was never Orvieto's worst problem. It was each other the inhabitants had had to look out for. At one time they had seriously considered abandoning the city as the only way to end their violence against one another. Yet the woman with the stroller was now leaning into the car that had stopped for her and her child. She was speaking to the driver. Both of them laughed as they talked. The baby sucked its fist and beat its heels against the base of its stroller. Just then thunder rumbled far away.

Unlike Isabel, Colin had imagined no one that afternoon. On the slow train from Florence to Orvieto he'd slept. While he slept, women of all ages walking through his car looked on him fondly. He was a few years younger than Isabel and although he was Canadian, he could have passed for European; he looked French, in dress as well as features. On arrival in Orvieto, he shuffled from train to funicular to bus between the elbows and umbrellas of the locals rather than waste time asking questions as Isabel had, which had meant she'd missed the first funicular. Otherwise, they would have risen together from the plains and the urban conglomeration at the foot of the cliffs to the medieval town. He would have seen her look relieved when the old contraption hurtling upwards at a seventy degree angle made it to the top.

The bus dropped him off in front of the striped Duomo. He set his knapsack down. Two tour buses and a van were parked on the diagonal across the square. He noted a public telephone on the steps of the building to the right of the Duomo, the tourist office, and a wine store. He had precise instructions for finding his lodging and did not (as Isabel did half an hour later) circle the wrong way around the big Duomo, bothering people in doorways with questions to which she could barely decipher the answers. He passed under arches and through ancient alleys without interest. He noted the money exchange, the cheap pizza places, and a laundry. He heard thunder before she did; he heard it while falling asleep in his room.

The book Isabel was reading was trying to persuade her that people were more callous in medieval times and more apt to act on impulse, however cruel. They had childlike personalities, the book said, and a childlike perspective, not only in their art.

She stood again at her hotel room window, thinking about those people, although she had her supper in a bag in her hands. Her window looked out on other windows, on rooftops corrugated with clay tiles, on stained stone walls and a cobbled street. A precarious looking iron shelf protruded from the window directly across from hers. Four clay pots, in which the earth was dry and the plants had long since died, leaned to the slant of the shelf. Below and to the left of the window was an arched doorway. Once no doubt it held a sturdy oak door; now it was barred with flimsy looking embossed steel. The new door emphasized the oldness of the city. It was hard to believe in a time when these buildings were new. Even harder to believe in their construction, in workers calling to one another as they mortared the walls, in young brides planning the first placement of furniture in rooms. Her book told her that the Middle Ages were a non-progressive time. For years historians hadn't wanted to study the period. It didn't fit with the way they wanted to think about the history of humanity. It was a disturbed time, the book said. The citizens of Orvieto walked the streets with their hands ready near their daggers. Woe to anyone involved in a family feud, woe to any Jew. Or any cross-cultural fornication. Any acts of love or lust between a Jew and a Christian were punishable by the death of the woman. She would be beheaded or burned alive. The book didn't say whether she'd have a choice or who would decide it.

And this was where Lodovico belonged. In a time when your neighbour would slit your throat over an insult. In a time when travellers were looked on with suspicion. And people were more suspicious than ever once the great pestilence, the Black Death, ravaged Italy like God's vengeance. Yet she saw Lodovico walk with purpose through the crowded streets of Orvieto and no one stopped him. When he passed, people stepped back out of his way. In the middle of a laugh or a shout, they skittered aside, their mouths open without sound. They averted their faces, even halted arguments to avoid coming into contact with him. His red robe and his red hood with its slits for his eyes allowed him to walk unassaulted among them.

The thunder came nearer. Isabel sat on her bed eating corn and sausage pizza and potato pizza glistening with olive oil while Lodovico stalked the streets. She licked the oil from her fingers. The Duomo bell tolled and she thought she could see ripples of sound rising past her window.

She had finished her dinner and was sipping her second glass of the cheap Chianti she'd carted with her, her version of coals to Newcastle, when the sky went black. Thunder rolled up to her window. She lay on her back in the dark room and watched lightning perform a fireworks display. Between the claps of thunder she heard people shouting at one another from windows and from the street as they scurried for shelter. Then rain pelted down. The stones of the old town bonged with sound and when lightning lit the sky, the rain could be seen, as near to solid as rain could be. Isabel allowed herself a third glass of wine as she always did in exceptional circumstances, which, with travelling, seemed to be increasing.

Colin woke to the storm. He woke hungry and was annoyed because he had declined dinner at his pensione. The electricity had gone off, so perhaps dinner would have been postponed or cancelled anyway. He could hear no one moving or talking in the apartments. He was inclined to feel a little better if he wasn't the only one doing without.

On his back in bed in his dark room, he reviewed the old memory of waking in the back seat of his parents' car, between his two sleeping brothers. And the windshield wipers going. Rain on the car roof. Streams of it sliding sideways as he looked into the night and fields ran past him, their edges illuminated by the headlights. In his room in Orvieto the shutters were closed. He didn't care how the rain fell.

Later he went out in search of food. The streets were bright and dark and crowded with people gadding about before dinner. He had to detour past old men in groups of three or four who scuttled along as one creature so as not to miss a single nuance of their animated conversation. He had to stop for boys and girls intent on making their way to other boys and girls congregated on steps, leaning against arches. He was trapped for minutes behind a mini-skirted woman in fishnet stockings who was escorting two older, black-clad women at a measured pace. The buildings dripped, gutters gurgled. Restaurants opened their doors and the owners stepped out to look hospitable. The pizza places were closed. It was time for serious dinner. The tourists slowed to read menus by lamplight and were seduced into a trattoria before making up their minds. He followed the largest number, but had a table to himself. The major portion of the tourist season was over, which made it easier for him to scan the faces.

Isabel was asleep before he walked back to his pensione. She was dreaming about buying a dress but could not decide which colour she wanted to wear.

Once he'd left the area near the main square, the streets were empty. And dark. On a street parallel to his, he heard the footsteps of a person wearing hard shoes. He was glad to be in runners; he would not have wanted to hear himself so clearly. The footsteps came toward him and soon the person turned onto his street, walking close behind him. Then, ahead, he thought he saw someone dart from one doorway to another. A car arced around the corner and bombed toward him. The street was narrow enough he felt compelled to stand aside with his back against a wall and then felt foolish. He continued on his way, walking faster. The footsteps were very close behind him. He had not liked to look at the person as the car passed, it had seemed too intimate a situtation, but afterwards he wished he had. At the door to his pensione, he half-turned as if to fumble for his key, but his follower had disappeared. He went inside with a smile on his face. The landlady smiled back, looking up at him from her ironing. She was listening to the radio. Someone was singing in English; he didn't recognize the song or the voice. The landlady spoke to him but he had to shrug and smile again. "Spooky town you live in," he said and it was her turn to shrug and laugh at what sounded like a joke.

He had slept too much to be tired. He plucked a book from his knapsack, but it lay unopened on the bed beside him. He drifted into a state that was closer to a trance than remembering, a state that had become habitual with him. He drifted back to his childhood. All his memories were of his childhood. He had mostly forgotten what he had done after the age of twelve. He thought maybe his father had been more influential than he knew, but it was his brothers who figured most importantly in his memories. His mother had tried several times to commit suicide. She had not been successful yet, but she had managed to erase herself from his consciousness, at least.

He had threatened suicide once. This wasn't one of his memories. It was simply written on his brain, a tattoo, so much a part of him that he was able to forget it. When he was seventeen, his father, a sergeant in the air force, took his last transfer to a base outside Montreal. Colin wasn't quite old enough or brave enough to refuse to go with his family, although it meant leaving his girlfriend of nearly two years and felt to him like having half his skin torn off. He and his girlfriend wrote back and forth for a while, in codes in case their mothers intercepted the letters. Then her letters got distant in tone; she dropped the codes. Then she stopped writing. He sent her a letter threatening to kill himself if she didn't write. She didn't write.

On his bed in Orvieto, he summoned memories of his brothers. He and his brothers, the three of them sticking together. Against their parents sometimes, against the bullies when they moved to a new base and that was necessary. With his brothers Colin had combed ditches for pop bottles and beer bottles. Yes, that was good to remember. That was the summer just after they had moved to Alberta. You could get into the movies every day on the air force base for a nickel. The three of them could gather a nickel's worth each in an hour. Then they met other boys, who joined them. Ten or twelve of them went out mornings hiking through the ditches around the base. They had to act tough to keep other kids from following them. It took longer, as it was, to collect enough. They pooled their findings and quit only when they had the price of admission for everyone. They hunted far afield and most days the hunt was more fun than the movies. They were a posse, searching for a glint of glass and finding much more along the way. They found dead mice, gophers, birds, a couple of times porcupines they had to keep their dogs back from. They found skeletons and more often skulls of dead things, lying like treasures in the tangled grass, and once a small deer, half-alive, that had bounced off somebody's bumper. They had raced back to the base, abandoning the hunt, and felt important reporting it to the military police.

Nothing made him special when he was a kid. He had never thought of himself as anything but ordinary. In the morning when he woke in Orvieto, he wondered if it could have been a woman's footsteps in the street the night before, but considered that unlikely.

Isabel had the best coffee of her life in Orvieto, rich with steamed milk. The coffee was served and apparently had been brewed by a small middle-aged man she hadn't seen in the hotel the night before. She exclaimed to him about its goodness. He nodded, but he was in a hurry to be out of the room. She was the only guest taking breakfast; she wondered if she was the only guest in the hotel. She supposed her presence in the dining room was interrupting something he was listening to on the radio or television. She imagined the kitchen behind the swinging door, efficient with stainless steel and the latest appliances. She had noticed that Italians delighted in fixtures.

Breakfast was dry rusks and melba toast and one delicious small log of bread which came in a basket with butter and several American packets of jam. She felt happy enough to try three kinds. They were only strawberry, grape jelly, and marmalade, but she hadn't been offered a selection for weeks, she had hardly eaten for weeks, and they all tasted good.

The square in front of the Duomo was nearly dry. Although it was October, the sun promised to be hot by noon. But there were corners and alleys in Orvieto the sun never reached and they gave off a dank, old smell all day. Isabel intended to do nothing but wander. If she stayed here for days she doubted she would enter the Duomo or the museums nearby or consult any maps of the city.

In her wanderings, in the heat of midday, she found a sign indicating she was travelling in the direction of Etruscan tombs. She could not remember who the Etruscans were, but she kept on. After half an hour of hot walking, she noticed she was increasingly being forced off the roadside by heavy traffic, and the roadside allowance was becoming increasingly narrow. At least she was progressing downhill. She didn't relish the idea of returning uphill the way she'd come; she continued, hoping for a bus stop.

Her descent took her along the sand-coloured cliff edges of the old town. The cliffs were bonily eroded. They reminded her of the pork hocks she'd seen served in Milan. The waiter had carried them through the restaurant held aloft on a plate like a city of bones. In places the cliff sides were scaffolded. Here and there, windows and doors had been set into the face of the rock and buildings grew out of it or merged with it. Sometimes she stopped on her way down and looked over the countryside, which was enveloped in a sunny haze. She was hot and tired but almost carefree. Except for the times when motorcycles or cars or buses headed straight for her, on curves they seemed unlikely to be able to emulate.

Then she was at the tombs. She walked into a garden area where a fat man sat sleeping on a bench under a trellis. She stood looking at him for a minute, then passed him quietly and wandered down into the grassy hillocks that were the sodded-over roofs of the tombs. Here the noise of the traffic was muted and the misty light lay unevenly along the surfaces. The air was cool and damp. She walked down the paths between the tombs, trailing vapours, she fancied, because the stone blocks reached only about five feet high, which put the lush green roofs at her eye level and the mist that rose from them at the height of her head. Her fancy might have taken her further; she could have entered a tomb, through one of their low doorways. She could have lain down on a skinny shelf where once someone had placed the body of a loved one – if she had been inclined, and she had no doubt some tourists had been inclined, and had done so, in spite of the moss and slime on the stone floors.

A gentle-looking man appeared on a wooden foot bridge. At the sight of him, the idea of that wood, warmed by the sun, appealed to her. She went to him and in her bad Italian tried to ask him who these people were that had built the tombs, and when they had lived. He answered her in formal English. He was an archeologist, working on further excavations. They stood on the bridge together, looking down on these excavations, where the past was divided by string into neat segments. He began to tell Isabel about the Etruscans. "Not medieval, were they?" she asked. He was shocked. "No, no. Before Christ. A much different time." But by then she was not listening, because she had seen her enemy walking in the tombs.

When Isabel left, Colin spoke with the archeologist. He let him run on for a while about his work and then asked him if he knew the woman who had just left.

"No, no," the archeologist said. His lips pursed.

"Interesting woman," Colin said.

"Excuse me please, I must return to my work." The archeologist left Colin alone on the bridge with his amusement. Isabel could be seen trudging back up the road the way she'd come. She was dumb in some respects; Colin had noticed this before. Dumb in her reactions. She thought only of getting away, not of the best route. Colin walked away from the tombs, past the sleeping fat man, and found a bus stop in minutes. He was in his room before Isabel was halfway home.

She took a long shower. She was ashamed of herself for running away, for being afraid when she had determined that was over. She went out for a restaurant dinner because she couldn't be alone in her room. She ordered pasta, veal, and a salad. Only one glass of wine. She ate so little the waiter asked if there was a problem with her meal. Ordinarily, she would have taken the opportunity to practice her Italian, but she waved him away with a shake of her head. Her mind was occupied with her enemy. She didn't try to summon her resources against him. Her resources were pathetic, nothing but whimsy, the kind a child might manufacture, against the fact of him.

She had seen him first in Milan. She hadn't paid him much attention, she had just been annoyed to find him watching her and grinning because she was marrooned on a traffic island for a long time. She had been trying to cross the street to the train station. Her bag and her knapsack were heavy, the traffic threatening. And then this guy was laughing at her. She was surprised to see him again in a shop in Venice where she'd gone to buy film. She almost convinced herself she was mistaken, that she had imagined a resemblance. But then he showed up almost everywhere she went in Venice. Twice he boarded the same vaporetto. She cut her stay short. Then he appeared in the doorway to the wine bar where she was drinking, in Florence. She turned her back on him, she panicked. She thought if it happened again she would have to confront him, but not now; she needed to be strong.

Only one glass of wine, yet when she left the restaurant she turned in the wrong direction. At first she didn't know she was lost. The night was chilly and she walked quickly. Then she noticed she was going down an unfamiliar street. She turned back to the last intersection she had passed. She could hear people on other streets but could see no one and really didn't know which way to turn. The streets were mere alleys, winding out of sight. She couldn't see into the darkness.

She made an effort to imagine that she belonged here, that she was comfortable on these streets. She thought of the tombs, of the fat man sleeping on the bench and the archeologist who had spoken to her in English. It had been comforting to hear English spoken again and to be able to speak it. She walked slowly, telling herself that the people of Orvieto would like her if they knew her. After all, she appreciated their fondness for fixtures. Nowhere had she seen more ingenious light switches or shower heads. And she was ready at any moment to declare her love for their food and their wine. She kept on, hoping she was making her way back to the restaurant, but she was walking more slowly now. She was afraid to deviate further from her hotel and afraid to think of standing still in the darkness.

A couple emerged from a doorway. The man had his arm around the woman as he ushered her to their parked car. When Isabel went to them, they pried themselves apart and were kind and helpful. In Italian, they directed her homeward and repeated the directions, waiting at each described turn for her to nod her head. *Sinistra, sinistra:* she had to keep turning left.

She found her hotel with no trouble. She looked up at its ugly stuccoed false front with affection. When she went inside, the woman behind the desk greeted her almost as if she considered her a friend.

Colin leaned in an archway. He was interested to note that she had chosen a tacky hotel and then seemed to admire it. The hotel was listed in the guide books, recommended as a second choice in its price range. He'd noticed she always took second-best; she avoided the hotels, restaurants, and sites the books extolled. Her coming to Orvieto and staying more than the recommended couple of hours was an example of this proclivity of hers. He wondered if she wanted more variables than perfection could offer or if she was afraid of being disappointed.

He pushed off in search of a bar. He wanted some place noisy, some place where friendly American tourists hung out. People who would slap him on the back. He was pretty sure he wasn't going to find it. This town was too small; it catered to the safer set, not the adventurous. Somewhere between Isabel's hotel and his pensione, he heard footsteps behind him, rapidly gaining on him. He guessed they were men, two or three of them. He stopped at a shop window, to pretend to look at lace, of all things, and let them pass him. Within minutes, he thought he was being followed again. Of course the streets of the cities of Italy were often crowded. You could not think you were being followed just because people walked behind you. Still, he gave up the idea of the bar and went back to his pensione.

He lay on his bed remembering the farms he had drawn as a child. He had never been on a farm but he had drawn a woman feeding chickens, a man milking a cow, a girl leading a horse, a boy hoeing a garden. He had drawn a barn, fences, trees, the sun in the sky. The farm in his imagination, as intensely coloured as it was on paper, had grown each time he'd drawn it. He'd entered the picture as he made it and when each drawing was full of people and their activities and nothing more could be added, he'd pulled out and felt nostalgic. It was interesting to him to think what a strong sense of nostalgia he'd had as a child. He would have thought it was an emotion for adults.

Isabel thought she heard a child crying. She was walking in the medieval quarter during that time after lunch when businesses were closed and the streets were deserted because the local people were resting. Without people in them, the streets displayed their oddities, or what seemed like oddities to Isabel: new plastic shutters at old windows, balconies where there were no doorways, Virgin Marys over lintels. Of course, Virgin Marys were not exactly oddities in the Pope's home territory. Her book said Christianity was the stumbling block to understanding the Middle Ages. In a secular age, the book said, people could not comprehend a time in human lives when religion's power created such a gulf between ideal and real or a time when every day was lived in the shadow of the Day of Judgement. A particularly gruesome exhibition of the Day of Judgement was said to be carved on the front of the Duomo in Orvieto. Isabel had not attempted to find it. She didn't want to view as a tourist a picture that once was real enough in the imagination to cause mortal fear, the kind of picture that had caused people to abandon the sick or hide from them, they were so afraid of dying and reaching the Day of Judgement unshriven. In those days of plague, when half the priests had died or run away, many of the people would have lived in fear of such a death.

Isabel had only cats for company on her walk. When she stopped before a slender archway, two of them darted at her, hoping she had food. She ignored them, hesitating because the alley beyond the archway turned into a footpath and she didn't like to invade anyone's private property. Further on, she saw more doors, so she went through.

The stone walls on the other side, in the denser shade, were gloomy. She was beginning to feel sad. She thought the weight of history was making her sad. She felt too alone; even the cats had left her. At the corner of a building which had been decorated with a splendid wrought iron balcony and many pots of geraniums, she thought she heard the child crying. She listened hard. She pressed her ear to the stone wall. She decided it must have been a subliminal form of hearing, if she had heard anything at all, but she stood waiting there.

The alley wound upward to a blind end and yet another stone wall; this one she estimated was eight or nine feet tall. It would have been there in that same spot in Lodovico's time. Someone else standing where she stood could have looked up the alley and seen him as she did now, standing with the wall behind him, a clouded sky above him. In his red hood and robe. He had just come out of the house at the top of the alley. She saw him stride without hesitation down the narrow path toward her, walking in a matter-of-fact way toward her while inside the building beside her, on the other side of the window set into the wall, a child was crying. Only a pane of glass and a yellow curtain separated her from Isabel.

The child lay on the window seat. Huddled on the window seat, a girl of ten or eleven. In a deserted house. She was crying because she was sick and alone. She had turned her head to the window. Rich yellow curtains, lustrous as sunshine, were drawn across the glass. In the same matter-of-fact way he'd approached Isabel, Lodovico walked over to the girl. She was dying. No need to look in her armpits for swelling. In any case, there was no cure.

She would not look at Lodovico. She kept her face turned from him, as she had been told she must, to prevent spreading her disease. She said her parents had left her. They had taken her younger brothers away in case she should look at them or breath on them and infect them.

Lodovico said to her, "They did not leave you alone. They sent me to look after you." This of course was untrue. He had never been to Orvieto before and didn't know who her family was.

"Are you not afraid?" she asked. He said she should not concern herself with his fate. He was a member of the Compagnia della Misericordia of Firenze; it was his duty to do what he could for her. He did not tell her that people were afraid of him, too, because he had touched the sick and now possibly contaminated others.

She was concerned for her soul. He told her about the Pope's blanket absolution during this time of plague. He didn't know whether or not the absolution had been made law, but he thought if she died believing it had, God would understand. He knew how close to heresy he was. She was not content, poor child, so he went the further step and said he had the power to pardon her, if she would have him for her confessor. With her eyes on the window hangings, she listed her small sins.

He turned her head toward him. She was damp with fever. Her eyes glittered. "Why do you wear that hood?" she asked.

"It is only for anonymity, so my acts will be anonymous."

"Will it hurt you if you take it off? If I look at you?"

"No, no. The sickness does not come from your eyes."

He removed his hood and held her hand and listened while she repeated Christ's words of redemption. Soon after that she died. He took down the yellow hangings to wrap her in. He did not take her body. He had given up trying to bury the dead.

Isabel left the medieval quarter. The streets were coming to life again. Everyone was walking to the main squares where the smell of pizza reminded her she hadn't eaten lunch. She bought herself two slices – one with artichokes and carrots, another with olives and peppers. Before she was out the cafeteria door, she absently started eating. She strolled along with the crowd, stopping when the people in front of her stopped. She looked into shop windows at wood carvings and pottery while they chatted with one another. When both slices of pizza were gone, she turned back and bought two more.

Colin meant to leave the medieval quarter. He took a wrong turning, which was not like him, but then the area was a warren of alleys and the buildings all looked alike. He had been irritated all day by the persistent feeling that he was being watched, that he was in some way a marked man, yet he hadn't been able to catch anyone watching him. He kept hearing footsteps behind him, even during the quiet afternoon hours, and when people came out again into the streets, he began to suspect he was being followed not just by one or two but by eight or ten or more. He speeded up, wanting to get into a main thoroughfare. He checked over his shoulder and saw that there actually was a band of Italian youths behind him now. They were walking more slowly than he was, watching him. He tried not to hurry too obviously away from them. They started making the throat-gurgling mocking lion's roar sound that had amused him when he'd heard it other times. It was a greeting or a code between them. They liked to think of themselves as macho guys.

He saw that he had made a mistake. He'd turned into a blind alley. They were close behind him, calling Rrrrr, Rrrr to one another and laughing. He turned, sweating, knowing that as soon as they saw his face they saw his fear. They yelled comments back and forth, grinning at him and advancing. One made a feint at punching him, another casually stuck his foot out as if to trip him, but they let him pass. They were content with enjoying his distress.

It was evening when Isabel crossed the square in front of the Duomo and encountered a gang of young men on the steps of the building where the public telephone was located. She had to wend her way between their motorcycles to make it clear she was standing in line. Though there was no line. The young men grabbed the phone from one another. They poked and shoved one another and danced around trying to shout each other down. Soon, though, her gravity subdued them and in a few minutes they drifted away. She called her son. One of his roommates answered and got him out of bed. She apologized for calling so early. He said it was all right, it wasn't early, he was just sleeping. He sounded glad to hear from her. He asked where Orvieto was. "An hour from Rome," she said. "You'll be going there next," he said, but she said she didn't think so. She said she was halfway through her travels and was getting tired. She didn't think she had the stamina for Rome and might stay here longer. He asked her what it was like. Not the kind of place you'd boast about discovering, she said, but she felt she belonged here for a while. She told him it reminded her of

Victoria, a city with a tourist image of itself. They had gone to Victoria together, once. She had given a paper at a conference. She didn't mention the trip to him; it had gone badly. The conference had been unpleasant, to say the least, and he had, at eleven, looked after her. When he said good-bye, he had that protective tone of voice he had perhaps first assumed then. She said good-bye with her gratitude held in check so he wouldn't worry.

She would have liked to stroll but was very tired. She passed the Duomo steps where a few girls had joined the boys. Some of the young people were already paired off and in each other's arms. She passed the lit restaurant where the well-to-do tourists were enjoying a quiet meal, and went down the steps, through the arches that led to her hotel.

He was waiting for her. He wasn't looking for her; he didn't know from which direction to expect her. But he was waiting, standing in an archway watching her hotel. By the time he heard her footsteps and turned, she was almost upon him, her face like a moon in the darkness. Her face appeared to him as he knew it would appear in any number of the photographs he'd taken – surprised again. Her anxious eyes peered at him from the dark shadows under the archway, looking for something in him. No wonder he prized her. Even caught off guard, she expected something, some reason or response. Just for a second he wanted her to find it. He wanted her to reach out her hand and put her finger on it. But he was already backing away, the camera to his eyes.

She was wearing a blue dress he hadn't seen in all the time she'd been travelling. Usually she wore jeans and a t-shirt, which was how he knew she was North American. Always afterwards, when he remembered her, she was wearing that dress. The sleeves and skirt were long and the fabric was a true blue, the colour of deep water. Or the colour of crayon a child would chose to illustrate water. Not one of those children adults have in their imaginations who colour the sky green and trees purple and are called creative, but a child who wants to get things right.

Something about her had intrigued him – he couldn't have said what it was – when he saw her in Milan, and he had followed her. He hadn't meant to let her see him. He'd simply wanted to capture selected moments in her travels. Some of the moments were admittedly trivial, yet they were all revealing. It was the first time he'd been seen at work and maybe he was going too far, maybe he should have stopped the project. But her seeing him had become an advantage, her anxiety a nice counter to her coolness. The results would be dramatic. Maybe she'd see the series some day and be flattered. He was getting quite well known. He had exhibited in Montreal and Toronto and had found his way into a small gallery in New York.

It had been mostly luck, keeping up to her the way he had. Such luck couldn't go on forever. At any rate, he had enough now – the dress made a fitting final image – and he decided in the morning he would take the train to Rome.

In her room, Isabel lay on her bed for hours, awake, until she decided where Lodovico was.

Lodovico was lying under the stars. He was camping out along the road from Orvieto to Firenze. He had made the long trip to find his sister, but he had been too late, she was dead before he reached Orvieto. He had prayed a priest was with her at the end so that she had not died unshriven. He prayed no longer.

The country was not peaceful, not even at night. Bands of brigands roamed the land, armed and reckless. With death at their heels, they plundered and killed. They had been exposed to the plague and were not afraid of Lodovico, but neither was he afraid of them.

Connie Gault writes fiction and plays. Her published works include the short story collection, *Some of Eve's Daughters* (Coteau Books), and two plays, *Sky* and *The Soft Eclipse* (Blizzard Publishing). Her work has also appeared in *Canadian Fiction Magazine*, *Grain*, *NeWest Review*, *Prairie Schooner*, and other literary magazines as well as anthologies such as *The Old Dance* (Coteau Books), *Lodestone* (Fifth House), and *Celebrating Canadian Women* (Fitzhenry and Whiteside).

Gault's plays have been produced across Canada and her radio dramas have aired on CBC and the BBC World Service.

"Inspection of a Small Village," the title story of this collection, received the Prairie Schooner Readers' Choice Award from the University of Nebraska in 1994. Gault has also won several Saskatchewan Writers Guild fiction awards. She is the current fiction editor of *Grain*.

Gault was born in rural Saskatchewan and has lived in Ontario, Quebec, Alberta, and British Columbia. She makes her home in Regina.